D0000037

I can't win, Enid told herself. *I just can't win*. Coming to the party had been a huge mistake. It was obvious that Jeffrey would *never* get over Elizabeth. Especially now that Elizabeth was so obviously leading him on.

Fighting back tears, Enid pushed her way through the crowd and out to the patio. She sank into a chair and tipped her head back. She felt more alone than ever. The distant noises of the party only intensified her feeling of isolation.

Why do I even try? she wondered. *What was the point of going straight and pulling myself together if this is where it gets me? At least before I was too stoned to notice how miserable life can be.*

As Enid sat by herself, gazing forlornly at the stars, a tear trickled down her cheek. The rest of the world was celebrating, and she had never been so unhappy in her life.

SWEET VALLEY HIGH

Super Star

ENID'S STORY

Written by
Kate William

Created by
FRANCINE PASCAL

BANTAM BOOKS
NEW YORK · TORONTO · LONDON · SYDNEY · AUCKLAND

RL 6, age 12 and up

ENID'S STORY
A Bantam Book / December 1990

Sweet Valley High is a registered trademark of Francine Pascal

Conceived by Francine Pascal

Produced by Daniel Weiss Associates, Inc.
33 West 17th Street
New York, NY 10011

Cover art by James Mathewuse

ISBN 0-553-28576-9

Published simultaneously in the United States and Canada

Bantam Books are published by Bantam Books, a division of Bantam Doubleday Dell Publishing Group, Inc. Its trademark, consisting of the words "Bantam Books" and the portrayal of a rooster, is Registered in U.S. Patent and Trademark Office and in other countries. Marca Registrada. Bantam Books, 666 Fifth Avenue, New York, New York 10103.

PRINTED IN THE UNITED STATES OF AMERICA

OPM   0 9 8 7 6 5 4 3 2 1

Dedicated to Jennifer Armstrong

One

"Finger, please!" Enid Rollins requested.

Her best friend, Elizabeth Wakefield, obediently put her finger on the knot, and Enid tied a bow around it.

"Hey, now I'm stuck!" Elizabeth pretended to struggle out of the knot and then sat back. "Thanks a lot! Now I'll have to go around with this Christmas present hanging off my finger!"

Enid nodded sadly. "And when people ask you to go out, you'll have to tell them you're all tied up."

Both girls burst into giggles. They were sitting on Enid's bed, surrounded by Christmas

1

wrapping paper, scissors, tape, and spools of ribbon. Christmas songs wafted from the radio.

"I love Christmastime," Elizabeth said, slipping her finger out of the knot as Enid tightened the bow. She sighed happily. "It puts me in such a great mood."

"You're *always* in a great mood!"

Enid looked at Elizabeth affectionately. Elizabeth was always wonderful to be with. She was a warm and friendly girl, the one person *everyone* at school really liked. There was a time when Enid had thought that she could never be friends with someone like Elizabeth Wakefield. When Enid was fourteen, she had run with a wild crowd. Back then, everything had revolved around cutting school, getting high, and goofing off. It had taken a bad accident with her then-boyfriend, George Warren, to make her see what she was really doing to her life. Going straight had been hard, but Enid had succeeded in putting the bad times behind her.

And it was lucky that she had been able to. So many of the kids she had known in the old days had dropped out of school or ended up in drug treatment centers. Now Enid was an A student in the junior class at Sweet Valley High, and unlike her old crowd, she knew that friendship, honesty, and love really mattered.

"You look pretty serious all of a sudden," Elizabeth said. "Those must be some deep thoughts going through your head."

"Not really," Enid said, smiling. She didn't want Elizabeth to think that she was getting all soppy and sentimental, just because it was Christmastime! She shrugged. "So anyway, what should we do over the vacation?"

"Sleep," Elizabeth replied immediately. She flopped backward on Enid's bed and gazed at the ceiling. "And because Todd will be in Utah skiing with his family until New Year's, you and I can do tons of stuff together."

Enid cut another piece of red-and-gold paper. "Aren't you disappointed about Todd being away at Christmas?"

Elizabeth made a rueful face. "Yes, I am, but there's not much I can do about it."

Todd Wilkins was Elizabeth's steady boyfriend. In Enid's opinion, they were the perfect pair. But secretly Enid was glad that Todd would be gone for a while. Enid didn't have a boyfriend at the moment. Recently she had broken up with Hugh Grayson. It would be fun to go shopping, see movies, and just hang out with Elizabeth. Romance was special, but so was best-friendship.

"But, Enid," Elizabeth went on, "I just remembered. What's the story on you and your mom going to Lake Tahoe? Do you have to go?" Enid's mother had planned on going to Lake Tahoe with Enid, to stay with her aunt. Then Enid's father had called up and said he wanted to spend Christmas with her.

Enid shook her head, setting her brown curls swinging around her face. "I told my mother that I wanted to spend time with my father. I mean, I love going to Tahoe and seeing Aunt Nancy, but I hardly ever get to see my dad."

"Did she understand?" Elizabeth asked. She sat up and began wrapping another gift.

"Well, she didn't exactly jump for joy," Enid said. "She and my father aren't on very good terms. I understand that. But he's still my dad, and I want to have a relationship with him."

"I can understand that your mom would be disappointed," Elizabeth said. "She was probably counting on having a vacation too. But you haven't seen your dad in ages, and it'll be great to see him at Christmas."

Elizabeth picked up a bow and placed it on Enid's head.

4

Enid grinned and shook the bow out of her hair. "Thanks for the support, Liz. And this bow is perfect for this present!"

"Hey, I was going to use that bow!" Elizabeth cried in mock dismay.

"Tough luck." Enid peeled off the tape on the back of the bow, then stuck it on the package in front of her. "So, who gets the neon-pink earrings?" she asked, pointing to a small unwrapped box.

Elizabeth held the huge pink hoops up to her ears. "Can't you guess?"

"It wouldn't by any chance be a certain twin sister of yours, would it?"

"How *did* you know?" Elizabeth answered. Her twin sister, Jessica, loved to dress in eye-catching clothes and unusual jewelry. She had such self-confidence that she was able to carry off the most outrageous outfits.

"What are you getting your mom?" Enid asked. "I haven't found anything for my mother yet."

Elizabeth rolled her eyes. "Me, neither. We'll have to go Christmas shopping as soon as vacation starts. I was thinking of buying her a silk blouse at Lisette's, but I'm not sure that I can afford it."

"I saw something really great at the mall the other day," Enid began. "It might be—"

Enid broke off suddenly as she heard her mother's footsteps in the hall. Her green eyes twinkled as she put one finger to her lips. Elizabeth nodded.

"Hi, girls," Adele Rollins said, poking her head into the room. "How's the wrapping going?"

"Great," Elizabeth replied. "We could do this professionally."

Mrs. Rollins chuckled, but then her expression became serious. "Enid, I just spoke to your Aunt Nancy, and she's really disappointed that we won't be going to Tahoe. I think you should give her a call yourself and explain the situation."

Even though Enid had already told Elizabeth about the situation, she wished that her mother hadn't brought the subject up in front of her best friend. "I will, Mom," she mumbled.

"Just because your father has to spoil our plans doesn't mean—"

"I said I will, Mom," Enid interrupted hastily. "I'll call her later."

Mrs. Rollins nodded. "All right, honey." She closed the door behind her as she left.

For a moment there was an awkward silence in the room. Then Enid said quietly, "You'd think she would let me see my own father without acting so grouchy about it!"

"Don't worry," Elizabeth said. "She'll get over it. Besides, don't forget about 'Peace on Earth, goodwill toward ex-husbands.' "

Enid looked up at her friend in surprise and then let out a laugh. "You know Liz, I'm really glad you're you."

Elizabeth smiled. "Now, we haven't talked about the most important thing of all yet."

"What's that?" Enid asked.

"What you are getting *me* for Christmas."

"A lump of coal!" Enid laughed as Elizabeth faked a scowl. No matter what was happening at home, Enid knew she could always count on Elizabeth to cheer her up. Having Elizabeth Wakefield for a best friend made up for a whole lot of unhappiness.

It was the last day of school before vacation. The students at Sweet Valley High were nearly delirious with excitement and anticipation. Enid had brought in a bag of chocolate candies, each one wrapped in red or green foil, and she was giving them out to all her friends.

"Candy delivery," she said to Winston Egbert and Maria Santelli and handed them each a piece of chocolate.

Winston, who was known for being the junior-class clown, instantly put his candy into his mouth without taking off the wrapper, and Maria screamed. "You dope! You can't eat that wrapper!"

Laughing, Enid continued down the hallway to her first-period class. Ms. Dalton, her French teacher, was putting a tape of French carols into the tape recorder on her desk.

"Are we having a real class today?" Aaron Dallas asked as he straddled a chair. "I mean, nobody's going to be able to concentrate for even five minutes."

"Mais oui," Ms. Dalton said, a slight smile on her face. "We're having a test today, and it will count for fifty percent of your grade."

A collective groan of agony went up from the students.

"Are you serious?" Amy Sutton demanded.

"No, of course not." Ms. Dalton opened the bakery box that was sitting on her desk. "I thought we would have a traditional French Christmas cake, a *bûche de noël.* No real work today, but, *s'il vous plaît,* try to speak French. That is, if you remember any."

"*Sí, señora,*" Aaron teased.

None of the teachers at Sweet Valley High really expected the students to work, so each class held its own holiday party. Enid had ginger cookies in history, chocolate meringues in math, and candy canes in English. By lunchtime, she couldn't think of eating another thing.

"I'm stuffed," she announced, when she sat down across from Elizabeth in the cafeteria. The group at the table was being unusually loud and boisterous.

"*You're* stuffed?" Elizabeth said. "I feel like I'm about to explode."

"Yuck, don't do it here, Liz," Jessica said. "This is a new sweater, you know."

Elizabeth tossed a candy wrapper at Jessica, and Enid giggled. The last day before winter break was nearly as fun as the last day before summer vacation. Not a single person could possibly be in a bad mood.

"Who's going to the skating party tomorrow?" Cara Walker asked the group.

"Me!" everyone chimed at once. The high school skating party was a new tradition, one that the students were hoping would become an annual event to kick off winter break. Each class had chipped in part of its funds to buy hot chocolate, marshmallows, and snacks.

"I have new skates." Jessica placed her arms above her head in a graceful arch. "Dorothy Hamill, look out."

Lila pointed at Jessica with one thumb. "Just because she can skate backward," she drawled. "Big deal."

"I can do camels, too," Jessica retorted. "You're just jealous, Li. You're still using those double-bladed skates, aren't you? I didn't know they came in your size."

Lila looked heavenward. The rivalry between the two friends was famous.

"Anybody bringing a hockey stick?" Aaron Dallas asked.

"It depends on who the hockey puck will be," Neil Freemount answered. "If it's Winston, I'll bring my stick."

Winston looked pained. "Please. I break very easily. Just ask Santelli." Maria swatted him playfully.

"I'm going to try a real jump this year," Amy Sutton put in. "I just hope I don't break an ankle coming down."

"Maybe I'll catch you," Bruce Patman, a rich and arrogant senior, suggested. He gave Amy a lopsided grin. "And maybe I won't."

Enid smiled and turned to say something to Elizabeth. But Todd had just pulled up a chair beside Elizabeth, and they were deep in conversation, their voices pitched low. Enid noticed a look of sadness on her friend's face. She knew it was because Todd was leaving for Utah right after school let out. She turned away again to give them some privacy.

"Who wants something to eat?" Winston asked.

A chorus of groans went up from the group. "Winston, you are the biggest pig!" Maria exclaimed. "How can you be hungry after all that junk food?"

"Just am," he said, shrugging his shoulders. "I'm a growing boy."

Laughing, Enid pushed her chair back and picked up her books. "I have to get going," she said. She leaned down to speak to Elizabeth. "See you later, right?"

Elizabeth and Todd looked up, startled out of their intimate world. "Sure," Elizabeth said, giving her friend a forced smile. "Since we don't have gym today, I'll meet you at your locker after the last bell."

"Bye, Todd," Enid said. "I hope you have a great time skiing, and Merry Christmas."

He smiled warmly. "Thanks, Enid. You, too."

As Enid left the cafeteria she decided that she would have to do something to cheer Elizabeth up. It was the least she could do, considering how many times Elizabeth had cheered *her* up. And by the end of the day, Enid had a plan.

Elizabeth's expression was somber when she walked up to Enid's locker. Enid had her jacket in her hand. She put it on, grabbed her bookbag, then slammed the locker shut and dialed the lock. "Did you drive to school today?"

Elizabeth nodded.

"Is Jess riding home with you?"

Elizabeth was beginning to look curious. "No, why?"

"Because I'm taking you somewhere."

"*You're* taking me somewhere, but *I'm* driving?" A bit of Elizabeth's usual sparkle lit her blue-green eyes.

"That's right," Enid went on breezily. "We're going to the Dairi Burger."

Elizabeth's mouth dropped open. "The Dairi Burger? Are you crazy?" She laughed. "I've eaten enough food today to last me until New Year's Eve!"

"Too bad." Enid looked Elizabeth squarely in the eye. "You're going to the Dairi Burger with

12

me, and there's nothing you can do about it. Do I make myself clear?"

Elizabeth smiled and shook her head. "I'm all yours."

"Good," Enid replied. "Now, let's get out of here. It's vacation!"

Two

Elizabeth tossed her book bag and jacket into the back of the Fiat Spider convertible she shared with Jessica. "Hop in."

"Why, thank you, ma'am," Enid drawled. "Let's hit the road."

Elizabeth climbed into the sports car and started the engine. She looked over gratefully at her friend. It was obvious that Enid was trying to cajole her back into the holiday spirit, and Elizabeth loved her for it.

She just hoped she *could* get back into the holiday spirit. The thought of spending the vacation without Todd made her feel lonely, in spite of Enid. Her relationship with Todd was one of the most important things in her life.

Just about the worst event that had ever happened to Elizabeth was Todd's family moving to Vermont earlier that school year. At first, she had thought that she would never get over losing him. After a while, though, she had started going out with Jeffrey French, and their relationship had been almost as wonderful. But then Todd had returned to Sweet Valley, and there was no denying how they still felt about each other. They couldn't *not* be together. After all they had been through, Elizabeth felt sad to be away from Todd at such a special, magical time of the year. She tried unsuccessfully to stifle a sigh.

"Not allowed," Enid said sternly. "No sighing."

"Enid!" Elizabeth laughed. "Boy, you're tough."

"Yeah, well, that's me, all right. Tough as nails."

"Yeah, sure," Elizabeth said. "Tough like a marshmallow."

She knew Enid was trying her hardest to cheer her up, and by the time they pulled into the Dairi Burger parking lot, Elizabeth actually felt a lot better. The girls got out of the car, linked arms, and started walking to the door.

Halfway there Elizabeth stopped. "I forgot my jacket. The temperature is always cold inside. Go ahead, I'll be right there."

While Enid went on, Elizabeth turned and jogged back to the car. She grabbed the light-weight jacket from the back and headed toward the Dairi Burger again. Then she faltered. Jeffrey French was also walking toward the door. They both stopped uncertainly.

"Hi," Elizabeth said, giving him a casual wave. Breaking up with Jeffrey had been hard, and she still cared about him as a friend. But some-times she felt awkward when they ran into each other unexpectedly.

Jeffrey's face lit up with his warm, familiar smile. "Hi, Liz. How's it going?"

"Fine," Elizabeth answered.

He held the door for her and followed her inside. Elizabeth immediately noticed a group of people watching them and smiling. Elizabeth and Jeffrey stood in the doorway, puzzled.

"Another pair!" someone shouted. "Two more victims!"

"What?" Jeffrey said under his breath.

"You guys are under the mistletoe!" Ken Mat-thews said and gave a hoot of laughter.

Elizabeth's heart felt as though it skipped a beat. She glanced quickly at Jeffrey to gauge his reaction. He was blushing slightly. Sure enough, a bunch of plastic mistletoe was hanging right above the doorway. They were trapped.

"Go on, French!" Winston called out. "What are you waiting for?"

"Kiss him, Liz!" Sandra Bacon, one of the cheerleaders, shouted.

Elizabeth and Jeffrey looked at each other. They would have to go through with the kiss if they ever wanted the teasing to stop. And besides, Elizabeth reasoned, it was totally innocent. There was no harm in kissing an old boyfriend under the mistletoe. She and Jeffrey could be mature about it.

"What can I say? It's tradition," Jeffrey said, giving an exaggerated shrug. He grabbed Elizabeth in a melodramatic embrace, bending her back over his arm.

"Wooo-ooo!" hooted the crowd. "Go for it!"

Elizabeth was so surprised and confused, she hardly knew what was happening. And then she was aware of Jeffrey's strong arms behind her back and his lips on hers. Applause broke out from the crowd as the mock passionate kiss went on.

Part of Elizabeth knew that it was only a game. But part of her felt excited, too. She struggled to stand up. Jeffrey pulled her upright, and they broke apart. Elizabeth's cheeks were flushed. Their eyes met again briefly before Elizabeth turned away. Her thoughts were in a whirl.

"Way to go, Jeffrey," a boy called.

"I do have a reputation to uphold," Jeffrey explained with a show of modesty.

"You were holding Liz up pretty well," Neil Freemount put in.

Elizabeth was grateful that the crowd was beginning to break into little groups. She didn't look back at Jeffrey, but instead wove her way among the maze of tables to the booth in which Enid was sitting.

"What was going on over there?" Enid asked. "I couldn't see what everyone was yelling about."

Elizabeth couldn't meet Enid's gaze. "Oh, it was nothing," she said distractedly.

"Then why do you look so guilty?" Enid said in a teasing tone.

"I do not—" Elizabeth gave an embarrassed laugh. "OK. Jeffrey and I came in at the same time, totally by coincidence, and we were standing under the mistletoe, so he kissed me. That's all that happened. It was nothing at all, really. No big deal."

Elizabeth realized that she was babbling, and she grabbed Enid's soda as a distraction. "Can I have a sip?" she asked.

"Sure," Enid said.

As she drank, Elizabeth let her gaze move quickly across the crowded restaurant. With a start, she realized that she was hunting for Jeffrey. She put the cup down abruptly and stared off into space.

Why am I acting so stupid? she scolded herself.

She couldn't deny the fact that she was rattled by Jeffrey's kiss. But it must only have been because she already missed Todd. She was just feeling lonely and sorry for herself. The kiss didn't mean anything.

After all, there was nothing between her and Jeffrey French anymore. Just because she could still remember how she once felt about him didn't mean anything. That was history now.

The roar of conversation was almost deafening. It seemed to Elizabeth as though nearly every student from Sweet Valley High was at the Dairi Burger, talking at the top of his or her lungs. Elizabeth was glad that it was noisy. She didn't feel like talking at the moment. "I'm getting a root beer!" she shouted as she got up from the booth.

There was another roar from the crowd by the door. Elizabeth stood on her toes to see who had just come in. Jessica was standing under the mistletoe, wearing a challenging grin. Lila and Cara stood nearby.

"Well?" Jessica asked. Her eyes twinkled daringly as she looked over the crowd of boys. She always got a kick out of flirting. So far, none of the boys had gotten up the nerve to kiss her. Then the crowd parted, and Bruce Patman sauntered toward her.

"Look out, Jessica," Lila said. "You're finished now."

"My dream come true," Jessica said. She clasped her hands together and fluttered her eyelashes. "Kiss me, you fool."

The crowd laughed appreciatively. Jessica and Bruce had dated for a short time, and as far as Jessica was concerned, it had been a disaster. Bruce was gorgeous, and he was rich. But he was also conceited. And Jessica didn't like going out with anyone who demanded more attention than she did.

Bruce's dark eyes locked with hers. "An early Christmas present, Jessica," he said in his typically arrogant way. He gave her a lingering kiss. Their friends let out a howl, and some of the boys started stamping their feet.

Just to be mischievous, Jessica had once said that Bruce kissed like a jellyfish. The truth was that Bruce was really a pretty good kisser. But

21

Jessica would have died before she would ever let Bruce know that! When they broke apart, Jessica patted her hair and said matter-of-factly, "On a scale of one to ten, Patman, I give you a seven point nine."

"I think you've got it backward, Jess," Bruce said smoothly. "What you meant was a nine point seven."

Jessica rolled her eyes. "I think I had it right the first time."

She reached into her purse and pulled out a candy cane, which she hooked on Bruce's shirt. "Merry Christmas."

"Come on, Jessica," Lila said. "This place is full of people in need of candy canes."

The girls had stopped on the way to the Dairi Burger to buy a big bag of peppermint candy canes. Jessica, Cara, and Lila thought of themselves as Santa's elves, delivering Christmas cheer. And Jessica knew that being Santa's helper provided a perfect opportunity to flirt with all of the best-looking boys. Jessica believed in taking advantage of all opportunities.

"Hey, Win," she said, hooking a candy cane on his ear. "How come you didn't kiss me under the mistletoe? I was counting on it."

"I wasn't—" Winston stammered.

Jessica smiled sweetly. "Oh, well. Maybe next

year. Merry Christmas!" She sauntered away, grinning. It wasn't as though she was interested in Winston; as far as Jessica was concerned, Maria was welcome to keep him. But Jessica loved to shake things up and make sparks fly.

She cruised around the tables, passing out candy canes and good-naturedly teasing everyone she knew.

"Have you been good this year?" Jessica asked Ken Matthews and Aaron Dallas. They both looked flustered, and Jessica gave them each a candy cane. "Well, you deserve a treat even if you've been bad."

Jessica found it extremely amusing to flirt outrageously. Boys were always so surprised. But that was because they were *just* boys. As far as she knew, she had dated all of the eligible guys at Sweet Valley High, and she thought they were all pretty immature. Jessica's ambition was to find a really terrific college man, someone handsome and sophisticated. Until she found him, however, she would make do with a cute high school boy.

Jessica stopped and studied the crowd. Suddenly her eyes lit on Jeffrey French, who was standing and talking to Neil Freemount and Penny Ayala. Jeffrey was one of the few good-looking boys at school whom Jessica *hadn't* dated. And that was only because he had started dating her sister almost as soon as he had moved to Sweet Valley.

But now he was extremely available.

"You have that devious look in your eyes, Jessica," Lila said, coming up beside her. "Who are you going after now?"

Jessica smiled archly. "Wouldn't you like to know, Lila Fowler." Jessica fought her way back toward the door and, after a few jumps, managed to pull down the plastic mistletoe.

Several boys begged her to give them a kiss as she passed, but Jessica ignored them. She walked quietly up behind Jeffrey, held up the mistletoe, and tapped him on the shoulder.

He turned around with a questioning look. As soon as he saw her, his eyes lit up in surprise. Jessica felt a thrill of excitement as she waved the mistletoe above their heads.

"You're trapped," she said, giving him her most dazzling smile.

"Oh—Jessica." Jeffrey laughed somewhat feebly.

"Right," she said, trying to ignore the sound of disappointment in his voice.

Jeffrey smiled and gave her a quick kiss on the lips. "Merry Christmas, Jessica."

"It seems like we never see each other anymore," Jessica scolded, wagging her finger at him playfully. "We used to be such close friends."

Jeffrey looked slightly embarrassed. He nervously raked one hand back through his hair. "Oh, well . . ."

"That was when you were going out with my sister." Jessica tapped him on the shoulder with the mistletoe. She wouldn't *really* want to date a boy her sister had been serious about, but she didn't mind flirting with him. "But now that you aren't anymore, it feels as if I've lost a friend."

"Yeah, well—" Jeffrey shifted uncomfortably. "I'll see you at the skating party tomorrow, right?" he asked, beginning to edge away.

Jessica curbed her impatience and gave him another melting smile. He didn't have to act as if she had the plague! "Great. I'm such a klutz on the ice. Maybe you can help me stay up." Jessica hated lying about her skating ability, but sometimes flirting required desperate measures.

"Sure." Jeffrey nodded quickly. "I'll see you then."

He walked away, and Jessica felt like an idiot. Cara, who had managed to find a booth, called to Jessica. "Over here, Jess."

Cara had been watching the scene between Jeffrey and Jessica, and as Jessica sat down, Cara said, "Wow, you really made a big impression on him." Her brown eyes sparkled with laughter. "You'll have to tell me your secret one of these days."

"It's my fatal charm," Jessica said.

She distractedly unwrapped a candy cane. Maybe she *should* try to start something with Jeffrey, she mused, snapping off a bite. Of course, she wouldn't want anyone to think she was taking Elizabeth's leftovers. But he *was* cute. There was no getting around that fact.

Unfortunately, there was no getting around the fact that, for a second back there, he had thought that she was Elizabeth. And he had looked happy. In fact, he had looked *thrilled* at the possibility.

But that could work in her favor, too, Jessica decided. If he couldn't have Elizabeth, why not have her identical twin? Jessica smiled. Maybe the best way for Jeffrey to get over Elizabeth was to console himself in Jessica's arms.

Someone sat down next to her and startled her out of her musing. It was her twin. "Hey, Liz."

Elizabeth helped herself to one of Jessica's candy canes. "Hi. What were you and Jeffrey talking about?" she asked casually.

"Nothing," Jessica replied. She studied her sister's expression for a moment. "Why?"

Elizabeth shrugged. "No reason. I just saw you guys talking, and I was surprised."

"I *have* talked to boys before," Jessica pointed out sweetly. "It's not that unusual."

"Oh, never mind." Elizabeth laughed as she stood up. "I'll see you later."

Jessica took another bite of her candy cane. She sure hoped this winter vacation was going to be interesting. So far, it didn't seem to be off to a very exciting start.

Three

Enid shook the ice in the bottom of her cup and glanced around to see where Elizabeth had disappeared to. As she looked over the crowd, she caught sight of Jeffrey. He waved to her and headed for her booth.

"Hi, Jeffery," she said. "How's it going?"

"Hi, Enid." He slid into the seat across from her, pushed up his sleeves, and leaned back. Then he sat forward again and began to fidget with the napkin dispenser.

Enid arched her eyebrows quizzically. "Something on your mind?"

"Oh, well—" Jeffrey met her eyes and smiled

sheepishly. "I was just thinking that I must have looked like a real idiot back there."

"Back where?"

"That mistletoe stuff—with Liz," he explained. "I know I shouldn't have made such a production out of it. Did Liz say anything? Was she mad?"

Enid smiled at him reassuringly. "Don't worry about it Jeffrey. She said that you guys got caught under the mistletoe, and so you had to kiss. She said it was no big deal."

"Yeah, well, I must have looked pretty dumb," Jeffrey said morosely.

"No way! I mean, I didn't actually *see* you, but there's no way *you* could ever look dumb," Enid insisted.

Jeffrey smiled.

Enid couldn't resist smiling back at him. Jeffrey was such a nice guy. Enid felt a bit sorry for him. She knew that he must have been devastated when Elizabeth broke up with him to go back to Todd.

"I just don't want Liz to be upset with me," Jeffrey continued.

"You still miss her, don't you?" Enid asked softly.

Jeffrey shrugged his shoulders and looked away. "No, that's over with."

Enid wasn't going to embarrass Jeffrey by making him admit it, but she was pretty sure that he still cared for Elizabeth. After all, he wasn't dating anyone else at the moment.

"So, how've you been, anyway?" Jeffrey asked brightly, obviously eager to change the subject. "It seems like a long time since we last talked."

"Yeah, it does," Enid agreed.

"I always think of you as a really good friend, Enid. I'm sorry that we don't spend time together anymore."

Enid smiled sadly. "I know. It doesn't seem very fair, does it? You shouldn't have to give up friends when a relationship ends, but that's the way it always seems to happen."

"You're right." Jeffrey propped his chin up on his fists. "Speaking of people I don't see much, are you still going out with Hugh?"

"No, I'm not seeing him anymore." Enid shrugged and leaned back in her seat. "Or anyone else, for that matter. What can you do?"

Jeffrey laughed. "Don't ask *me*. I'm certainly not the expert." His expression was serious for a moment, and then it brightened.

"Speaking of experts—you know what? You're just the person to give me some help. I'm going out of my mind trying to find a Christmas gift for my mother. Got any ideas?"

"Well . . ." Enid thought for a moment, then said, "does she like perfume? Silk scarves? Kitchen utensils? Books? Gift certificates from her favorite store? Magazine sub—"

"Whoa! Hang on!" Jeffrey broke in. "I've got to write these down. Got a pencil?" he asked as he pulled a napkin from the dispenser.

Enid laughed and opened her shoulder bag. She pulled out a pen. "Here you go."

Jeffrey began to write furiously. "OK, I'm caught up to magazine subscriptions," he announced. "What else?"

"How about one of those fancy cake stands that spins around and plays a song? You probably can't get one that plays a Christmas carol, but how about 'Happy Birthday?'"

Jeffrey looked up from his writing and grinned. "She already has one of those. Any other ideas?"

Enid couldn't keep from giggling. "Gee, let me think."

"Do you think she'd like one of those corny T-shirts that says 'World's Best Mom'?" Jeffrey asked. "Or maybe one that says 'Don't Talk to Me Now, I'm Having a Crisis'?"

"Yeah, any mother would love that one." Enid laughed.

As Enid watched Jeffrey, she thought, *I'd forgotten how cute Jeffrey is.* He was also fun to be

32

with. It really was too bad that just because he wasn't dating Elizabeth anymore, he and Enid couldn't be friends. Not that there really was anything or anyone preventing them, but things just hadn't worked out that way.

Enid tried to concentrate on something besides Jeffrey's adorable smile and the way his thick blond lashes framed his eyes. "My mother always loves it when I make her something myself."

He looked skeptical. "It's a little late for that, isn't it? Christmas is only four days away."

"Well, you could give her a gift certificate worth a certain number of dinners that you'll make," Enid suggested. "Or a certain number of windows that you'll wash, a certain number of times you'll do the food shopping for her. You know, offer her something that will make her life easier."

"That's a great idea," Jeffrey said enthusiastically. "My mom's always saying that feminism just means a woman gets to have *two* careers—one inside and one outside the home!"

Enid held out her hands and smiled. "There you go. With a gift like that, she'll probably think she's gone to heaven."

Jeffrey handed back Enid's pen. "I have to admit, Enid, you're brilliant." He leaned forward. "And you're right about something, too. There's no reason we can't be friends. Let's do something together. You're going to the skating party tomorrow, right?"

"Right," Enid said.

"Great!" Jeffrey said. "Then why don't we go together?"

"Sure," she said. "That sounds good."

"Can I pick you up tomorrow morning about ten?"

"Ten is perfect." Enid was still smiling as Jeffrey walked away. She knew that he had asked her to the skating party as a friend, and that was just fine. Enid really did think of him as a friend. And it was nice to know they could still spend time together in spite of what had happened with Elizabeth.

"I'm back," Elizabeth announced, suddenly sitting down in the booth. "Sorry I was gone so long. I was telling Penny about a Hemingway book I read last week."

"That's OK," Enid said. She hesitated. She wanted to add, "I had company," but then Elizabeth would want to know who, and Enid would have to say that it was Jeffrey. Not that there was anything wrong with that, but after what had happened under the mistletoe, Enid decided not to mention it.

Elizabeth leaned back in the booth, the cheerful expression slowly fading from her face. Enid watched her for a moment. In spite of the rowdy atmosphere at the Dairi Burger, Elizabeth was beginning to look wistful.

"I'm ready to leave any time," Enid said.

Startled, Elizabeth looked at her friend. "I'm sorry—I guess I'm just out of it today."

"That's OK." Enid gave Elizabeth a warm smile. "It's too noisy in here, anyway. I can only take so much enthusiasm."

"All right," Elizabeth agreed.

When they were seated in the car, Elizabeth hesitated for a moment before turning on the ignition. "Enid?"

"Yes?" Enid asked.

Elizabeth shrugged one shoulder in a preoccupied way. "I was thinking. Do you want to go shopping tomorrow morning? Maybe even drive up the coast to some of those little towns that have interesting boutiques?"

"But—" Enid broke off. She had just been about to tell Elizabeth she was going to the skating party with Jeffrey. And there was really no reason not to tell her. But something held her back. It would be awkward, that was all, Enid reasoned. No need to trouble Elizabeth about Jeffrey when her friend had so much else on her mind.

"Oh, I forgot," Elizabeth said hastily. "The skating party. I just don't feel like going. Did you want to go?"

Enid nodded without looking at her friend. "I was planning to," she admitted.

Elizabeth smiled and started the car. "That's OK. I'll go shopping by myself. We can do something later on in the day."

To her surprise Enid was relieved to hear that Elizabeth wouldn't be at the ice rink. Now Enid wouldn't have to explain why she was there with Jeffrey.

"Well, if you're feeling down, maybe you just need some time alone to think," Enid said, feeling a little dishonest. "You probably wouldn't even have fun at the party."

"I know. I probably wouldn't," Elizabeth said.

"And besides, maybe Todd will call tomorrow." Enid stared steadily out the window, wishing she could shut up. She knew that she was trying to find reasons why Elizabeth should miss the party, and she knew that what she was doing was pretty crummy.

They were silent for the rest of the ride. When Elizabeth pulled up in front of Enid's house, Enid took a deep breath.

"Listen, Liz, forget what I said about having time alone to think," she said earnestly. "If you're sad and lonely about Todd being gone, being alone will only make it worse. Come to the skating party. It'll really be fun.''

Elizabeth smiled. ''Thanks. But I think I'd rather not. I'll get some more Christmas shopping done tomorrow. After all, it's not like I don't see everyone all the time!''

''True.'' Enid laughed. ''But call me, OK? I don't want you being depressed.''

''I'll be fine.'' Elizabeth promised. ''Bye.''

As Elizabeth drove off, Enid let out a sigh. Half of her really wanted Elizabeth to go to the party. And half of her was very glad that she wouldn't be there. Wouldn't it just make Elizabeth sadder to see her best friend having fun with her old boyfriend when she herself was so lonely? But Enid couldn't really convince herself of this. She hated this feeling of disloyalty.

She turned and went into the house. ''Hi, Mom!'' she called out as she put her books on a living room chair.

''Hi, I'm in the kitchen.''

Enid walked to the back of the house. Her mother was sitting at the kitchen table, sorting through the mail.

''You just missed a call from your father,'' Mrs. Rollins said.

Enid's face lit up. ''Dad? What did he say?''

''Nothing,'' her mother said. ''The conversa-

37

tion ended when I told him that you weren't here."

"But did he leave his number?" Enid's father traveled often on business, so she was never sure where he might be calling from. For all she knew, he could be anywhere between California and New York.

Mrs. Rollins opened a bill. "No."

"Did he say when he would call back?" Enid pressed, trying to keep the disappointment and impatience out of her voice.

"No, he didn't, and I didn't ask," Mrs. Rollins said, getting up from her seat at the kitchen table.

Enid felt a lump come to her throat. "Mom," she began unhappily, "why do you have to act like Dad's so terrible? Can't you be nice to him at all? I mean, why couldn't you have taken a message or gotten his number?"

"I'm sorry, Enid"—Mrs. Rollins appeared to be agitated—"but I had just walked in the door, I had had a terrible day at work, and I just didn't feel like getting into a long conversation with him. That's all."

Enid turned away, feeling hurt and confused. She was positive that her mother had said something mean to her father. Enid felt a wave of sympathy for her father. He had called to talk to his only child, and he'd gotten an earful of crabby complaints instead.

"Do me a favor, Mom," she said. "Next time he calls and I'm not here, get his number, if it's not too much trouble."

Mrs. Rollins yanked open the refrigerator door and began to take things out for dinner. "I said I'm sorry, Enid. But you know that I find it difficult to talk to him after what he put me through."

Enid stared at the floor. "Oh, really? You never actually tell me about any of those supposedly awful things he put you through."

Her mother turned and looked at her. "Enid, you know perfectly well what I'm talking about."

"About how he supposedly has this big drinking problem?" Enid demanded. "*I* never saw him drink too much. I think you just exaggerated."

Mrs. Rollins shook her head wearily. "Let's not talk about it now," she said quietly. Enid could read the anger in her rigid back.

"I'll be upstairs," Enid muttered. "In case anyone calls and wants to talk to me."

When her mother didn't answer, Enid strode angrily out of the kitchen.

Winter vacation was getting off to a pretty rocky start.

Four

Elizabeth woke the next morning with a tingle of anticipation. Vacation! Christmas!

And then she remembered that Todd was away. She let out a sigh, rolled over, and covered her head with her pillow.

As Elizabeth lay there feeling sorry for herself, there was a boisterous knock on the door.

"Go away," she groaned.

"Too late!" Jessica barged into her sister's room, flung open Elizabeth's closet, and began to search through her clothes.

Elizabeth sat up and glared at her twin. "Can I help you with something, Jess?"

"I don't have anything to wear to the skating

41

party," Jessica announced. She pulled Elizabeth's light blue snowflake sweater off a shelf and began to put it on over her pajamas.

"Is that how you ask to borrow my clothes?"

Jessica's head popped through the neck of the sweater. "Who are you? Scrooge?" she asked, her eyebrows raised. "Liz, you're breaking my heart. How can you be so grumpy? It's Christmas vacation!"

"I am not grumpy," Elizabeth retorted. When she heard the sound of her own voice, she hesitated. "Well . . ."

Jessica bounced onto Elizabeth's bed. "You know what your problem is?"

"No, but I have a feeling you're going to tell me."

"Your problem is that you think you're not allowed to have any fun when your boyfriend is away."

"That's not true!"

"Yes, it is." Jessica grabbed Elizabeth's hands and dragged her out of bed. "You're getting up, and you're going to the skating party with me." Suddenly Jessica let go of her sister's hands, and Elizabeth flopped onto the floor. "Ow! Thanks, Jess. I'm really awake now."

"Well, don't just lie there on the floor like a

bum!" Jessica cried out. "Get up! Take a shower! Find your skates!"

When Jessica got going, she was like an unstoppable force of nature. With a laugh, Elizabeth stood up and stretched. Why *shouldn't* she go to the skating party? she thought. It was stupid to waste her vacation sitting at home. Feeling sorry for herself wouldn't bring Todd back any sooner, and he would feel terrible if he knew that she was in self-imposed isolation.

"OK, OK, you win," she agreed. "I'll go skating. But I want my snowflake sweater."

Jessica stuck out her tongue. "Traitor," she muttered as she stripped off the sweater and flounced back to her own room.

Still smiling, Elizabeth sat down at her desk and took out a piece of stationery. At the top she wrote, "Dear Todd," and then she sat thinking for a moment. Finally she began to write.

It's the first day of vacation, and I already miss you a lot. It won't be like Christmas without you. But I know you're with your family, and I really hope you're having a great time.

Anyway, I hope you get this before Christmas. I just wanted to tell you that I love you, and I miss you, and that I hope you have a wonderful Christmas. I'll be thinking of you.

Love, Liz

Elizabeth propped her chin on her hand and gazed off into space. Then an image of Jeffrey's handsome face popped into her mind. Elizabeth shook her head confusedly, quickly picked up her pen, and added a big "XXOO" after her signature. She knew that she was only thinking of Jeffrey because she had been so lonely the day before. And then that crazy mistletoe episode had taken her totally by surprise. Just because she thought of Jeffrey while writing a letter to Todd didn't mean she was being unfaithful, she reminded herself.

I'm going to have fun today, she told herself firmly. *And not think about anything at all.*

After breakfast, a shower, and a frantic wardrobe session with Jessica, Elizabeth headed down to the basement to find her skates. "Got 'em!" she yelled up the stairs.

"Then let's go," Jessica hollered back. "Quit wasting my valuable time."

"Valuable time," Elizabeth snorted, giving Jessica a swat on the arm. "Come on."

On the way to the rink, Elizabeth and Jessica

tried unsuccessfully to sing "Jingle Bells" as a round. Elizabeth continually got confused, and Jessica accidentally threw in a chorus of "Deck the Halls." By the time they began the "Jingle Bells, Santa Smells" version, they were both laughing too hysterically to continue.

"We could cut our own album," Elizabeth said. *A Wakefield Family Christmas.*"

"You mean *A Wakefield Family Disaster*," Jessica corrected her.

Once at the rink they spent a few minutes greeting other Sweet Valley High students. Then they took off their shoes and laced up their skates. When Jessica disappeared into the ladies' room to brush her hair, Elizabeth stood by the railing and watched the skaters gliding by. She waved to people she knew. A lot of students had turned out for the event. With music filling the air and the colorful figures going around and around, Elizabeth was reminded of a carousel.

Elizabeth caught a glimpse of Enid skating around toward her. There was no mistaking Enid's bouncy brown curls, but because there were so many people in her line of sight, Elizabeth could not see who her friend was skating with. As they came closer Elizabeth recognized Jeffrey. Her heart started pounding faster.

Enid and Jeffrey were laughing. Enid was pretty wobbly on her skates, and her feet kept threatening to shoot out from under her. It seemed that only Jeffrey's arm around her waist kept her from toppling headfirst. Skating that way made them look like a couple. Jeffrey said something in Enid's ear that made her throw her head back and laugh.

A hot flush washed over Elizabeth's face. Then Enid caught sight of her friend and broke away from Jeffrey. He skated on without her.

"Liz!" Enid gasped, catching on to the rail. Her cheeks were pink, and her eyes glowed. "I thought you weren't coming."

"I changed my mind," Elizabeth replied slowly. She looked out at the crowd of skaters. "Did you and Jeffrey come together?"

Enid looked slightly sheepish. "Oh, well, we were talking about the party yesterday afternoon at the Dairi Burger, and he offered to give me a ride, that's all."

"You talked about it yesterday afternoon?" Elizabeth repeated. "At the Dairi Burger?"

"Well, yes," Enid said. "But there's nothing going on between us, Liz. You know that Jeffrey and I are just friends."

Elizabeth nodded. She knew that she had no right to grill Enid, but somehow she couldn't help herself. And if there was nothing going on between Enid and Jeffrey, why hadn't Enid mentioned their conversation on the ride home? If their relationship was perfectly innocent, there would be nothing at all to hide. It seemed now to Elizabeth that Enid looked very guilty.

"Liz?" Enid said in a concerned tone. "You aren't upset that I came with him, are you?"

"It's not that," Elizabeth said, straightening the cuffs of her blue sweater. "I just don't see why you had to hide it—that's all."

Enid frowned. "I wasn't *hiding* anything."

"But you didn't exactly tell me the truth, either." Elizabeth was breathing hard. "That's what hurts, Enid. And then you made such a big deal about my not coming to the party today. You obviously didn't want me to know you were coming with Jeffrey."

"Liz—" Enid drew a deep breath and forced Elizabeth to meet her eyes. "Jeffrey is not your boyfriend anymore. I don't think that you should get so upset."

Elizabeth felt a twinge of embarrassment. She realized that she was making a fool of herself and for absolutely no reason. "I'm sorry," she said, putting a hand on Enid's arm. "I guess it's just a gut reaction—you know. Old boyfriends,

47

that kind of thing. It's none of my business. Forget it."

"It *is* your business, Liz, don't say that," Enid said sympathetically. "We're best friends, and you're right, I should have mentioned that I was coming with Jeffrey. But, to be honest, I thought something like this might happen, that you might be upset, and I figured that because you were kind of in a down mood . . ."

"I know. I'm a dope," Elizabeth said. She tried to laugh. "Sorry to be such a pain. Listen," she went on, glancing over her shoulder, "I want to find Jessica. See you later, OK?"

"Well, OK. See you on the ice." Enid pushed off and skated clumsily away.

Elizabeth stood for a moment, watching her friend and wondering if Enid was looking for Jeffrey. Then she shook her head. It was none of her business.

Jessica had found Lila and Amy, and the three of them were skating together. Then Jessica turned and began to skate backward gracefully.

"Did you see that guy over there with the red sweater?" Jessica asked Amy and Lila, nodding her head to their left. "I think he's been looking at me."

Amy was skating with her arms crossed behind her back. "He's got a girlfriend," she said.

"How do you know?" Lila demanded.

"I saw them skating together before," Amy said, pleased with herself for knowing something her friends did not.

Jessica grimaced. "That doesn't necessarily mean anything," she said. But she decided to pass on the boy with the red sweater anyway.

Lila began to brag about the expensive presents she was expecting for Christmas. As the only child of the richest man in Sweet Valley, Lila was very spoiled.

As far as Jessica could tell, for Lila, Christmas was just another bonanza in a year of bonanzas.

"We were going to go skiing in Zermatt this year," Lila said. "That's in Switzerland, you know. But now Daddy has to make some megadeal in New York City."

Amy's gray eyes gleamed. "So you're going to New York?"

"No," Lila said. "Who wants to go *there* in December, anyway? It's freezing."

Jessica looked closely at her friend. "So what *are* you doing on Christmas? Will your father be home?"

"It depends," Lila replied, "on how the deal

49

goes. Daddy's a fabulous negotiator, and when he gets going, he doesn't stop for anything."

Lila was proud of her father's business acumen. Still, Jessica knew that Lila could not be too thrilled about spending Christmas alone with the housekeeper at Fowler Crest. Jessica decided to ask her parents if she could invite Lila to spend Christmas with them. After all, they *were* best friends.

Suddenly, Jessica caught sight of a tall boy skating gracefully along the rail. He had wavy brown hair and a great build, and he seemed to be keeping to himself. Jessica felt a little spark of interest.

"You guys," she said in a speculative tone, "check him out."

Lila looked closely at the boy. "Hey, I know who he is," she announced.

Jessica pivoted on one skate and fell into place beside her friend. "OK. What's the scoop?"

"His name is Brian something," Lila said. "He went to Big Mesa High, but now he's in college. University of Colorado."

Jessica smiled. "The rugged individualist, right? That's just my type."

"The whole male sex is just your type," Amy retorted.

Giving her friends a cheerful wave, Jessica

veered away to skate along the rail. Brian was just ahead of her. She smoothed her hair, put on her best smile, and speeded up. As she passed beside him she started to wobble and grabbed his arm.

"Oh!" she gasped.

"Hey!" Brian said. "Watch out!"

Up close, Jessica thought, Brian was just as cute as he had looked from a distance. "I'm *so* sorry," she said. "I'm the biggest klutz in the world. I just can't stay up for anything."

"You look as if you can do all right." Brian smiled.

Jessica felt a thrill of excitement. "I can do all right if I have some help," she said boldly. "Can I hold on to your arm until I get my stride?"

"Sure, no problem." Brian held out his arm, and she took it. "What's your name?" he asked.

"Jessica," she replied. Another dangerous wobble made her hold his arm a little more tightly. She could feel his muscles tense through his ski sweater. Brian was definitely a hunk.

"My name is Brian," he replied. "I know it's a real cliché, but, do you come here often?"

Jessica laughed. "No, not often. My school is sponsoring a skating party today. That's why it's so crowded. Kid stuff," she said, as though the party were the most juvenile thing in the world. "How about you?"

"I go to school in Colorado," he began. "So, I'm not in Sweet Valley very—"

"Look out!" someone cried behind them.

Before Jessica could turn around, someone plowed into her, and she went sprawling onto the ice. "Oww!" she groaned.

Jessica looked up to see who the clumsy jerk was. It was Enid. Jessica tolerated Enid because she was Elizabeth's best friend, but she had never been overly fond of her.

"I'm really sorry, Jess," Enid said, looking extremely embarrassed. "I couldn't stop."

"Yeah, sure," Jessica grumbled, still expecting Brian to help her up. But to her irritation Brian was looking intently at Enid.

"Don't you remember me?" he asked Enid. "Brian Saunders?"

Enid was blushing. "Sure I do, Brian. Sorry about running you over." She began to edge away.

"Wait," Brian said. "How've you been? I haven't seen you in a long time."

Enid's blush deepened. "Fine. Sorry again, Jess. Bye." Enid skated unsteadily away, and Brian watched her go, a look of disappointment on his face.

"Say, could you give me a hand?" Jessica asked sarcastically. She was very annoyed that Enid had smashed into them, and even more annoyed that Brian was so obviously interested in Enid.

Brian blinked and looked down at Jessica as though he had forgotten all about her. "Oh, sorry." He held out his hand.

"Thanks a lot," Jessica muttered as she struggled to her feet.

"Well, I'll see you around." Brian waved and skated away.

Stung, Jessica stood and watched his back. *How do you like that?* she thought.

But Jessica's exasperation was soon replaced by curiosity. Even though Enid clearly knew Brian from some other time, she had been very anxious to get away from him and to avoid conversation. Why would anyone run away from a gorgeous hunk like Brian?

Jessica spotted Lila and Amy and decided to rejoin them. The next best thing to flirting was gossiping, and she knew that her friends would be very interested to hear about what had just happened.

Five

Enid leaned against the rail for a moment to catch her breath. Running into Brian Saunders had been a real shock. She had known Brian back in the days when she was hanging out with a wild crowd. Her past friendship with Brian Saunders was one Enid definitely did not want to rekindle.

The friendship that interested her much more now was the one with Jeffrey. Enid could not believe what a good time they were having together, and she regretted even more that they had fallen out of touch.

"Hey, there you are," Jeffrey called out as he

skidded to a stop like a skier, sending out a splash of ice shavings.

"Show-off." Enid laughed.

"I'm trying to impress you." Jeffrey skated backward in a small, tight circle around her. "I don't have many talents, but I *can* skate. And you're getting the hang of it, you know. Another hour or so and you'll be skating like—like—who's that famous ice skater?"

"Katarina Witt?" Enid searched her memory. "Dorothy Hamill?"

Jeffrey shook his head. "No, that one from Sweden or Norway who made those funny black-and-white movies in the thirties—Sonja Henie!" He laughed. "That's her name."

"I saw one of her movies on TV once," Enid said. "You're right. It was so weird. All of the actors were on ice skates! Really goofy."

Jeffrey and Enid started skating together as they talked, their arms linked. Jeffrey looked down at her and smiled. "So that's who you'll be skating like. Sonja Henie."

"You think so, huh?" Enid said with a grin.

Enid matched her strides to Jeffrey's, and she was pleased to notice that she really was getting better. As they skated arm in arm Enid suddenly remembered an article she had read in *Ingenue* magazine. The article had asserted that if two people did something perfectly in synch, they were probably very compatible, which was certainly a good omen for romance.

Still, one thing kept nagging at the back of Enid's mind: Elizabeth. Since their conversation earlier, Elizabeth had been skating with other friends and somehow always managed to be on the opposite side of the rink. Enid wondered if it was only her imagination or if her friend was really avoiding her. Enid shrugged off the worry. She was there to have fun.

After another hour, Enid's ankles were wobbling back and forth. "I think I'm done in," she said to Jeffrey.

"Ready to go?" Jeffrey asked her.

"I think so," Enid admitted. "I have a feeling I'll be pretty sore tomorrow." She looked out over the rink but did not see any sign of Elizabeth. Enid had hoped to say goodbye to her friend.

Jeffrey and Enid changed into their shoes and left. As they drove back to Enid's house, they continued the easy bantering they had begun at the skating rink. They were both laughing when Jeffrey stopped the car in front of Enid's house.

"Listen," Jeffrey said, smiling warmly. "Let's

do something later. Do you want to see a movie tonight?"

"Sure," she agreed. "I sort of want to go to that new horror movie, but I'm such a chicken. I don't know if I could really go through with it."

Jeffrey's eyes lit up. "I really want to see that, too. Hey, I have an idea. You can cover your eyes at the gross parts, and I'll tell you what's happening."

"I'll probably miss the whole movie that way." Enid giggled. "But I'm willing to give it a try."

"Good." Jeffrey's green eyes danced with laughter. "Just don't eat a big dinner. You might lose it."

Enid pretended to gag and got out of the car.

She could feel the smile on her face as she watched Jeffrey's car disappear. Being with Jeffrey had been a lot of fun. They got along really well. And Enid had to be honest with herself. She was beginning to feel more than just friendship for him. She liked him. She liked him a lot.

In fact, Enid had liked him from the very beginning. When Jeffrey moved to Sweet Valley from Oregon, Elizabeth had tried to fix them up. But Jeffrey had had a mind of his own! He had fallen for Elizabeth, and Elizabeth had fallen for him.

Enid had not minded at the time because she hadn't had strong feelings for Jeffrey. But now . . .

Frowning, Enid stuck her hands in her pockets. What would Elizabeth think if she and Jeffrey started dating—started being more than just friends? If her reaction at the skating rink was any indication, Elizabeth would not exactly be happy about it. And Enid could understand Elizabeth's feelings, up to a point. But Elizabeth no longer had any claim on Jeffrey. Their relationship was over. There really was nothing to stop Enid and Jeffrey from dating.

Still, Enid did not want to risk hurting her best friend's feelings. And, of course, she had no real reason to think that Jeffrey even thought of her in that way at all. Judging by his manner so far, Jeffrey considered Enid a good friend, and nothing more. She was probably getting herself all worked up over nothing.

"Oh, forget it," she muttered, heading for the front door. *When the situation comes up—if the situation comes up—I'll deal with it then.*

That evening Enid got ready to go to the movies with Jeffrey. She had some extra time before Jeffrey picked her up, so she decided to wrap the Christmas present she had bought for

Elizabeth. It was a heart-shaped pink satin box trimmed in white lace. Enid knew her best friend would love it. She had just finished taping on the bow when the telephone rang. Enid paused, listening to her mother answer it downstairs.

"Enid! Telephone!"

From the sound of her mother's voice, Enid guessed that it was her father. She raced down the hall and grabbed the extension in Mrs. Rollins's room.

"I got it!" she yelled.

"Hi, sweetheart," Mr. Rollins said jovially.

"Hi, Dad! Where are you?" Enid asked, curling up on her mother's bed with the phone cradled against her ear. "When are you getting to Sweet Valley?"

Her father chuckled. "Why? Do you actually want to see your old man?"

"You know I do! I haven't seen you in so long!"

"Well, your mom isn't exactly thrilled about my coming. Is she still upset about cancelling the trip to Tahoe? When I spoke to her yesterday, she sounded a little cool."

"I think she *is* still upset about cancelling the trip. But I told her it was more important that I see you."

"Don't be too hard on her, sweetie."

Enid smiled. Her father was willing to stick up for her mother, but her mother would only criticize her father.

"I'm really excited about seeing you, Dad," Enid said softly.

"I'll be in Sweet Valley tomorrow evening," he told her. "I'm not sure what time, though. I'm driving in from Las Vegas."

Enid was surprised. "Las Vegas? What are you doing, playing the roulette wheels or something?"

"No, not at all, honey," Mr. Rollins said. Enid could hear the tinkling of ice through the phone as her father sipped a drink. "I had to meet some people here. Business. But enough about me. How are you?"

"I'm OK, Dad," she replied hesitantly. "I'm just really looking forward to seeing you. We have a lot to talk about—"

"Enid!" Mrs. Rollins called out.

Irritated, Enid covered the phone with her hand. Her mother always found a way to interrupt her when she was talking to her father. "What, Mom?"

"Your friend Jeffrey is here!"

"Oh! Dad, I have to go. Call me tomorrow?"

"I will, honey. Soon as I get in. Hugs and kisses."

"Hugs and kissed to you, too. Bye Dad."

As she hung up Enid realized that there was a lot she wanted to talk to her father about. But right now Jeffrey was waiting for her.

Enid ran back to her room, grabbed her shoulder bag, and hurried downstairs. Jeffrey stood up when she walked into the living room.

"Hi," he said, giving her a big smile.

Enid dropped her gaze. There was no kidding herself. She was beginning to feel more than just friendship for Jeffrey French.

"Let's go," she said quickly. "I don't want to miss any of the blood and gore."

When they got into the car, Enid suddenly felt shy.

"What have you been up to since the skating party?" Jeffrey asked.

"Wrapping presents," Enid replied. "I was doing Liz's just a minute ago."

Jeffrey looked interested. "Oh, yeah? What did you get for her?"

"Something really frilly and frivolous," Enid said. "A heart-shaped satin box. I found it at a store called Feminine Mystique. I always feel sorry for the guys who go in there. They look so embarrassed by the lacy nightgowns and things!"

"I bet Liz will like it, though," Jeffrey said.

"She likes to pretend that she doesn't go for that kind of stuff, but she really does."

"I know. She would never want to be seen as self-indulgent."

"I got her one of those perfumed things once. A sachet."

"Oh, I love those!"

"Liz really liked it, too," Jeffrey said.

Was it Enid's imagination, or was there a hint of wistfulness in Jeffrey's voice as he spoke of Elizabeth? For a moment, Enid wondered if Jeffrey still hoped for another chance with her best friend. She knew that he missed Elizabeth, but she didn't really think that he wanted her back.

Enid glanced at Jeffrey's profile as he drove. The headlights of oncoming cars highlighted his face, and she had to admit that she found him very cute. Jeffrey turned his head and gave her a friendly smile. Enid blushed and looked away.

You idiot, she thought. *Don't start getting any stupid ideas.*

"You're not going to embarrass me, are you?" Jeffrey asked in a teasing voice.

"Wh-what?" Enid faltered. Did he mean by falling in love with him?

"At this movie," Jeffrey went on. "If you're

going to scream or faint, you'll have to sit by yourself."

Enid shook her head, relieved that he hadn't guessed her thoughts. "No, I promise not to do anything embarrassing."

"Good." Jeffrey chuckled and looked over at her again. "You know, Enid, it's really great that we can still be friends."

Enid returned his smile faintly. "It sure is."

So Jeffrey thought of her only as a friend. But that didn't mean that his feelings wouldn't change. Enid relaxed against the seat and smiled in the darkness. Maybe there was something to wish for this Christmas, after all.

Six

Enid woke up the next morning with her mind made up. If she wanted something romantic to happen between her and Jeffrey, she had to make it happen—or at least give it a little nudge in the right direction. After having spent a wonderful evening with him, first at the movie and then at the Dairi Burger, she knew that she was right to take the chance. And Enid was sure that she could sort things out with Elizabeth, if and when she and Jeffrey became a couple.

Enid decided that she would give Jeffrey a Christmas present and watch how he reacted to her gesture. His reaction would tell her if there really was a chance for them. And Enid had a strong feeling that there was. She hummed as she strolled into the kitchen.

"Mom, can I use the car this morning? I have to do a little last-minute Christmas shopping."

"Last minute is right," Mrs. Rollins said, smiling. "Tomorrow is Christmas Eve. But you do still have time to get me that gold and diamond watch I keep asking Santa Claus to bring me."

Enid tipped her head to one side. "Mom, I hate to tell you this, but it's just not in my budget this year. Sorry."

"Oh, well. How about the Rolls-Royce?" her mother asked hopefully.

"Oh, that. They're just installing the TV and the cellular phone." Enid grinned. "That'll be ready for you. Don't worry."

As Enid was getting ready to leave, the telephone rang. She paused at the door to see if it was for her.

"Enid!" her mother called. "It's Liz!"

Enid ran to pick up the extension in the kitchen. She had not spoken to Elizabeth since the skating party, and she was glad that her friend had called.

"Hi," she said. "What's up?"

"Not much," Elizabeth replied. "What are you doing today?"

Elizabeth sounded a little bit lonely, and Enid's

heart went out to her. "I'm going shopping," she said. "Come with me."

It suddenly didn't matter to Enid that she had been planning to buy a gift for Jeffrey. Elizabeth was her best friend, and she wanted to cheer her up if she could.

"Oh, I don't know," Elizabeth replied. "I'm kind of sick of fighting the crowds."

"Then how about going to the beach?" Enid suggested.

Elizabeth sighed. "No, thanks. I just wanted to say hello and to see how you're doing."

"Sure you don't want to come?" Enid pressed.

"No, thanks. I'll talk to you later." Elizabeth hung up.

Enid sat by the phone for a moment. She knew only too well what it was like to feel lonely and blue. She knew that she couldn't force Elizabeth to cheer up and sometimes it was best just to be left alone. All she could do was to be available for her friend.

On the way to the mall, Enid thought about the skating party and the evening with Jeffrey. She wished she could go skating with Jeffrey every day of the vacation so that she could have a good excuse for holding his hand!

The mall's parking lot was crowded, and Enid had to park some distance from the stores. As she walked toward the mall, she thought about what she would buy Jeffrey. She had no idea what it would be, but she was sure that she would know it when she saw it.

Enid stopped by a huge selection of funky sunglasses. Maybe a pair of them would make an amusing gift. She turned the pivoting rack to see more of the styles.

"Hey!" a voice said indignantly. "I was looking at those!"

"Sorry." Enid peeked around the rack. "Oh, hi, Jessica."

Jessica was wearing a pair of bright green sunglasses. The top rim was decorated with miniature pink palm trees. "Oh, hi, Enid," she said, sounding less than thrilled. "What do you think of these?"

"I don't know," Enid said. "Those palm trees will probably break off after a week."

Jessica pulled off the sunglasses and jammed them back onto the rack. Why did Enid have to be so sensible all the time? she wondered. Enid and Elizabeth were exactly alike that way. "Probably," she muttered. Then she turned back to Enid with a conspiratorial smile. "Hey, I wanted to ask you something."

"Yes?" Enid asked.

"That guy Brian Saunders, from the skating

rink?" Jessica began. "He's really a hunk and a half. What's he like?"

Enid's cheeks were flushed as she looked intently at the rack of sunglasses. "Oh, I don't really know him that well," she stalled, putting on a pair of glasses so that Jessica could not see her eyes.

"He acted like you guys used to be friends," Jessica went on. "But you hardly even said hello to him before you took off."

"Yeah, well, I was in a hurry," Enid said evasively. "We were never really friends."

For a moment Enid was tempted to lay it all out for Jessica. *He's bad news*, she wanted to say. *When I knew him he was really messed up*. It was obvious Jessica was interested in him, and Enid did not want her best friend's sister to make a big mistake.

On the other hand, talking about that part of her life was both embarrassing and painful. And Jessica was the last person in the world she would want to discuss the details with. Telling Jessica something private was as good as making an announcement on the nightly news.

"Are you interested in him?" Jessica asked bluntly. She was watching Enid's expression closely.

"No, I'm not," Enid said. "And listen, don't waste your time on him, Jessica. He's not what he seems."

"Oh, really?" Jessica didn't look at all impressed by Enid's warning. "So, who are you shopping for? I thought you were the type who did all her Christmas shopping by Thanksgiving."

Enid decided to ignore Jessica's rude remark. And she decided to ignore the question, too. She didn't want Jessica to know she was shopping for Jeffrey, for the same reason she didn't want to talk about Brian. It was none of Jessica's business.

"Just a few stocking stuffers," she said, removing the sunglasses and turning away.

"Going to George and Robin's party tomorrow night?" Jessica asked quickly.

It was typical of Jessica to ask something like that, Enid reflected. Enid and George Warren had gone out for a long time, and Jessica obviously assumed that Enid was still jealous of Robin Wilson. Enid was glad that she could smile without a trace of insincerity.

"Sure. I wouldn't miss it for anything." Enid gave Jessica a casual wave and walked away.

Jessica's questions about her relationship with Brian Saunders had temporarily rattled Enid. Now she vowed to put everything out of her head except Jeffrey. She was going to concentrate on finding him the perfect present.

After another hour of shopping, Enid hit the jackpot at Reel Revival, a store that sold Hollywood memorabilia. In a rack of black-and-white postcards, she found a picture of the figure skater Sonja Henie. Enid smiled as she thought about the message she would write on it. And she would get a box of candy to go with it, she decided. Better, a carton of ice cream to go with the skater. Pleased with herself, Enid bought the postcard and headed home. Even the memory of her run-in with Jessica Wakefield couldn't spoil her good mood.

When Enid arrived home, her mother was sitting at the kitchen table going over the year-end bills. "Did anyone call?" Enid asked her mother cheerfully.

"Not a soul, Enid."

"Dad didn't call?" Enid pressed. She felt a little disappointed.

"I said, *no one* called," her mother answered curtly as she signed a check.

"OK, OK." Enid leafed through the Christmas cards that had come in yesterday's mail. Most of them were from people Enid didn't know, and that made her a little sad. Sometimes she felt that she and her mother were drifting further and further apart, their lives becoming more separate all the time.

The phone rang. "I'll get it," Mrs. Rollins said, lifting the receiver. "Hello? Oh, she's right here."

Enid saw a flicker of stubborn irritation flash across her mother's face. She held her hand out wordlessly and passed the phone to Enid. No matter how her mother felt, Enid was determined to be cheerful for her father.

"Hi, Dad! When are you picking me up?" she asked.

Her father chuckled. "Gee, honey. I wish it could be right now."

"Why don't you?" Enid asked, turning her back to her mother.

"Sorry, Enid. I'm calling from the road," he explained. "I'll be in town pretty late, but I want to make a date with you. How about having lunch with me tomorrow? And afterward we can go clean out the stores."

Enid giggled. "Let me check my calendar," she teased. "Yes, that day is open. I'll pencil you in."

"Great. How's your vacation going so far? Having a good time?" he asked.

"Sure, Dad," Enid said.

"Good. Why don't you come to the hotel at noon? I'll be at the Sweet Valley Regency."

Enid grinned. "Pretty fancy, Dad."

"Just a place to throw my bedroll," Mr. Rollins drawled in a cowboy voice. "See you at twelve o'clock, right?"

"Twelve o'clock," Enid repeated. "See you tomorrow."

Enid hung up and let out a happy sigh. Then she noticed that her mother was staring at her. "What's wrong?" Enid asked.

"Are you seeing him tomorrow?" Mrs. Rollins asked. "At twelve in the afternoon?"

"Yes," Enid said. "What's wrong with that?"

Mrs. Rollins threw her pen down on the table. "Well, that's just terrific. I bought us matinee tickets to *The Nutcracker.*"

Enid gulped. "Oh, no!" she said, genuinely upset. "You never said anything about it."

"It was supposed to be a surprise," her mother said. "Great. First he ruins our plans for the vacation, and now he ruins this, too. We're supposed to just drop everything when he feels like coming around, is that it?"

Enid felt angry and weak at the same time. "He's my father!" she said, her voice unnaturally high. "You don't want me to spend any

73

time at all with him, do you? Do you really think I'd rather go to the ballet than see him?"

"No." Mrs. Rollins snapped her checkbook shut and gathered up the bills and envelopes. "I guess it was foolish of me to make any plans at all with him around. I should have known he would find some way to spoil them."

"Mom, you're not being fair," Enid said, trying to control her voice. "He's not trying to spoil anything, he just wants to see me!"

Mrs. Rollins shook her head. "His timing is awful, as usual."

"When *would* be a good time, Mom?" Enid asked. "As far as you're concerned, I don't think there'd *ever* be a good time."

Her mother let her breath out slowly and then said, "Honey, I'm sorry I flew off the handle like that. I know he's not doing it on purpose."

"He's not," Enid agreed. Her throat was tight with tears. She knew that the divorce had been hard on her mother, but it had been hard on her, too. It had been hard on all of them.

"And it doesn't matter about the show," Mrs. Rollins said. "I won't try to come between you and your father anymore."

She gave Enid a swift hug and hurried out of the kitchen. Enid stared into space. Why did everything have to be so difficult? she wondered.

The telephone rang again, startling her out of her reverie. She looked at it for a moment before picking it up.

"Hi, Enid? It's Jeffrey."

Instantly Enid smiled. At least there was one bright spot in her life this vacation. "Hi, how's it going?"

"OK. Listen, are you busy right now?" he asked.

"Now?" Enid was pleasantly startled and a little bit flustered. Her hand automatically went up to her hair. "Well, no. I guess I'm not doing anything. Why?"

"Well, would you like to come over? I wanted to ask you something, and the party at George's tomorrow won't really be the right place," Jeffrey said. His voice sounded very intimate.

Enid was thrilled. The invitation was just what she had hoped for. She suspected that he might have a gift for her, too. It would be the perfect time to exchange them, when they were alone.

"Sure, that would be great," Enid replied casually, trying to contain her excitement. "I'll be over in about twenty minutes, OK?"

"Great," Jeffrey said. "I'll see you then."

After she hung up the phone, Enid drew a

deep breath, clenched her fists, and drummed her heels excitedly on the floor. This was her chance! Enid ran upstairs to her room. One look in the mirror told her that she had to change: blue jeans and a pink T-shirt wasn't exactly her prettiest outfit. She rapidly skinned off her jeans and shirt and then put on a white turtleneck and a swingy red skirt. With a green headband pulling her hair back, she was the embodiment of the Christmas spirit.

Hmm. Am I too dressed up? she wondered, studying her reflection in the mirror. No, she decided. Holidays were for dressing up, after all. And she did want to make a good impression on Jeffrey.

Enid took out the black-and-white postcard of Sonja Henie and looked at it for a moment. Remembering how Jeffrey had teased her about her skating made her smile. All she had to do now was to buy a pint of ice cream on the way to his house. She sat down at her desk, picked up a pen, and scrawled "To an admiring fan, from Sonja" on the back of the card. She laughed, then jumped up for another critical look at herself in the mirror.

"Don't get your hopes up, Rollins," she commanded herself sternly.

But it was no use. Her heart told her that

something really special was happening between her and Jeffrey. Sure, it might only be wishful thinking, but wishing could sometimes make a dream come true.

Enid paused just long enough to dab a little perfume behind her ears. Then she grabbed Jeffrey's postcard, put it in an envelope, and raced downstairs. She could hardly wait to see him.

Seven

Enid's heart pounded with anticipation as she knocked on Jeffrey's door. In five minutes everything could be different between them—she could feel it. If there had been stars out, she would have wished upon one. Starting a new romance would be just the thing to make her feel better about her parents. She drew a deep breath to steady her nerves.

"You're here," Jeffrey said as he opened the door. He noticed the carton of ice cream she was carrying. "What's that for?"

"Christmas present," Enid said, handing it to him. The card was on top. "It all goes together," she explained shyly.

Smiling, Jeffrey stood back and let her in. "This is great," he said as he led the way into the living room. A big Christmas tree with cheerfully blinking lights filled one entire corner of the room. No one else seemed to be at home, which made Enid feel even more hopeful and happy.

Enid smiled eagerly as she watched Jeffrey take the card out of the envelope. A smile spread across his face as he looked at the picture, then turned it over to read the caption. He let out an appreciative chuckle.

"This is great," he said. He leaned over and kissed her on the cheek. "Thanks."

Enid's pulse raced, and she dropped her gaze bashfully. "I thought you'd like it," she said.

"I do. I love it." Jeffrey laughed. "I'll put it up over my desk upstairs. Want some ice cream?"

"No, thanks," Enid replied. She felt too nervous to eat anything.

Jeffrey stood up and went over to the Christmas tree. "I've got something for you, too," he said, reaching into the pile of presents.

When he handed the package to her, Enid tried to think of something to say. But her mind was a blank. All she could think about was how warm and soft his lips had felt against her cheek. She carefully unwrapped the present and turned it over. It was a book.

"*Sonnets from the Portuguese*, by Elizabeth Barret Browning," she said. "That's wonderful!" She opened the front cover to see if he had written an inscription inside. It was blank. She tried not to feel let down.

Jeffrey was smiling. "I'm glad you like it. I thought you would. Liz always talked about how much you like poetry, so I took a chance that you didn't already have this collection."

"It's great." Enid couldn't help wondering, however, if Jeffrey had given her the book because Browning was Elizabeth's favorite poet. She was sure that he hadn't done it deliberately, but perhaps he had chosen the book subconsciously, because of his attachment to Elizabeth. After all, he had gone out with her for quite a while. If Enid and Jeffrey were going to spend a lot of time together—and Enid was hoping they were—she was willing to pay the price of dealing with Jeffrey's past relationship with Elizabeth.

Jeffrey sat down on the couch and leaned forward, his elbows on his knees. Enid held her breath.

"Enid?" Jeffrey began. "Can I ask you something?"

"Sure," she said calmly. "Ask me anything."

He smiled at her warmly. "Thanks. The thing is, Liz brought me some Christmas cookies this morning, and I just thought, well—" He broke off.

Enid's smile was frozen on her face. Elizabeth hadn't mentioned anything about baking cookies for Jeffrey when she had called that morning.

"Do you think that means something?" Jeffrey blurted out. "I mean, do you think she still cares about me, and that's her way of saying it?"

"I don't know," Enid said. Her mind was spinning. Why would Elizabeth have brought Jeffrey a Christmas present? It didn't make any sense. And Jeffrey thought that it meant something. Didn't he think it meant something for him to have exchanged presents with her?

Jeffrey stood up and began to pace. "I'm probably just getting my hopes up for nothing. Has she said anything to you about me?"

The hopeful look in Jeffrey's eyes made Enid's heart plunge. He wasn't interested in her at all. He was still in love with Elizabeth. She had been a complete fool. Enid shook her head mechanically.

"Liz hasn't said anything at all to me about you," she said hoarsely.

"Because I really need to know," Jeffrey went on. "If I thought—well, I don't know. But bringing me a Christmas present must mean something, don't you think?"

Enid nodded, a sympathetic smile plastered on her face. Obviously, Jeffrey still thought of her simply as a good friend, someone he could turn to for advice. She had blown the whole relationship way out of proportion. When she thought of how close she had come to embarrassing herself, she cringed.

But Enid gave no sign of her pain. "I really don't know," she said, trying to sound supportive. "She might have made cookies for a lot of people."

"But she said that she made them just for me!" Jeffrey replied.

Why? Enid asked herself. What was Elizabeth trying to do? Why was she keeping Jeffrey hanging on? Was it because Enid was spending time with him? She couldn't believe her best friend was acting this way. It just wasn't like Elizabeth at all.

No matter what Elizabeth's motives, however, one thing was perfectly clear. Jeffrey had no intention of falling in love with Enid. He still hoped that Elizabeth would come back to him. Enid felt a wave of resentment against him. She knew she hadn't imagined all the good feelings between them. He had misled her into thinking that he might care about her as more than just a friend. And now that Elizabeth had brought him a Christmas gift, he had dropped Enid in a second.

She frantically scanned her memory for a time when she might have said something that had revealed her feelings for him. She couldn't think of a thing. At least she hadn't made a fool of herself.

Enid was beginning to tremble. She knew she couldn't stay there much longer pretending to be sympathetic to Jeffrey. She had arrived with such high hopes, and they had all crumbled around her.

"I really don't know how she feels about you," Enid said in a carefully controlled voice. "Maybe you should just ask her yourself."

"You think so?" Jeffrey sat down and tapped his fingers on his knees while he thought. "I don't know. It doesn't seem right."

Enid stood up abruptly. She had to leave before the situation got worse. She felt hurt and confused. "I have to go," she said.

"You do?" Jeffrey seemed genuinely disappointed. But that was only because he wouldn't be able to ask any more questions about Elizabeth, Enid told herself bitterly.

"Yeah, sorry," Enid replied. "My mother needs the car."

"Maybe we can do something later," Jeffrey suggested. "If you're not busy."

Enid clenched her jaw. Jeffrey's invitation was tempting. But would he just use their time together to talk about Elizabeth? There was nothing wrong with being pals, but she had wanted and expected so much more. A romance with Jeffrey would have made everything else in her life so much easier to take. Now that romance wasn't going to happen, she didn't know whom to blame.

"Maybe," she said, heading for the door. "I'm not sure if I can. Give me a call."

"I will. Thanks again for the ice cream," he said cheerfully. " 'Bye."

Enid hurried outside and climbed into the car. For a moment, she sat, staring ahead. What had just happened was like a nightmare. Her chin trembled slightly as the pain began to sink in. *You were dreaming, Enid,* she told herself sadly.

All of the nice things Jeffrey had said to her,

all of the hopes she had built on them—none of them meant anything at all now that Elizabeth had interfered. Elizabeth and her Christmas cookies had ruined everything.

Enid started the car and headed for Elizabeth's house. She was determined to ask her just what she had been thinking when she brought Jeffrey those cookies. Elizabeth *must* have said something that made Jeffrey start to feel hopeful, and Enid wanted to know what it was and why Elizabeth would want to encourage Jeffrey when she claimed she loved Todd.

But as she turned down Elizabeth's street, Enid slowed to a stop. If she barged in and demanded to know what Elizabeth was up to, Elizabeth would know that she was interested in Jeffrey. And after insisting at the skating party that she wasn't, Enid would look like a liar and a hypocrite. The whole situation was just a terrible mess. She felt she had been treated very poorly, even though she knew she was responsible for letting her hopes get too high.

After a moment, Enid turned the car around and drove home. The worst part of it was that she couldn't go to her best friend about the problem.

Elizabeth *was* the problem.

*   *   *

Enid was comforting herself with a cup of hot chocolate and watching *White Christmas* on TV early that evening when the phone rang. She carried her hot chocolate into the kitchen to answer the phone. It was Jeffrey.

"You know what we should do?" he said in his usual friendly tone. "We should go to that new go-cart track that just opened. I'll race you."

I'm just one of the boys to him, Enid thought. Well, she wasn't going to be one of the boys anymore. She could still salvage some of her self-respect.

"No, I can't," she said, keeping the hurt out of her voice. "I forgot to tell you before that I'm doing something with my mother tonight." It was a lie, but she didn't care.

"Oh." Jeffrey sounded a bit disappointed. "Oh, well, some other time. You're going to the party tomorrow night, though, right?"

Enid stared into her hot chocolate. "I'm not sure yet. Maybe."

"I'll call you tomorrow, then. OK?"

"OK. Bye."

When she hung up, Enid ran through the conversation again in her mind. He had sounded disappointed. Was it because she had turned him down? Or because his buddy Enid was too busy to give him more advice about Elizabeth?

Enid walked back to the living room and set her hot chocolate on the coffee table. She sat down and angrily punched the pillow next to her.

"You jerk," she muttered, addressing herself and everyone else in her life.

Enid stared at the TV and sank even deeper into gloom. It was already getting dark outside, and the only light in the room came from the television screen. Fighting with her mother, waiting and waiting to see her father, striking out with Jeffrey, being angry with Elizabeth—Enid felt completely alone.

Then the telephone rang again. Sighing, Enid got up and went into the kitchen to answer it. She just hoped it wasn't Jeffrey, calling back.

"Hello?" she said.

"Enid? It's Brian Saunders."

Enid was so startled that she could not even say hello.

"It was really great running into you yesterday," Brian said. "Even though *you* ran into *me*. How have you been? I haven't seen you in a long time."

Enid finally recovered her wits. "I'm OK," she replied guardedly.

"I was thinking, maybe we could get together," he went on. "Do you want to have dinner tonight? Celebrate the holidays?"

"I don't hang out with the old crowd these days, Brian," Enid said calmly, hoping he would understand that she meant she didn't party anymore. Enid was proud of the fact that she had pulled herself out of that mess. In fact, at the moment, that pride seemed like the only positive factor in her life. "I'm totally straight now."

Brian laughed. "That's great, Enid. I'm really glad to hear it."

"You are?" Enid was skeptical. When she had known Brian, he had been very wild, and also very scornful of anyone who was not.

"Look, I know I used to be pretty out of control," Brian said, as though reading her mind. "But that was back when I was just a kid. I've really changed a lot."

"Yeah?" Enid was skeptical.

"Yes, I have," Brian insisted. "People can change, you know. You changed, didn't you?"

Yes, she had. Enid knew that it wasn't impossible for someone to change. Still, it was hard to believe that someone like Brian . . .

"Well . . ." she began hesitantly.

"Listen," Brian cut in. His voice was smooth

and assured. "I'm in college now, and that has really straightened out my priorities. And when I saw you yesterday, I remembered how much I always liked you. It's just that back then, I was so wasted all the time, and you were with George."

Enid felt flattered in spite of herself. "You liked me?" she asked.

"Are you kidding? You were always so friendly and funny," Brian said. "I'm just really glad I got the chance to see you again. You're—you're not dating anyone now, are you?"

"No," Enid replied. "I'm not going out with anyone."

"Then you'll have dinner with me?" Brian asked.

"I don't know," she said slowly.

"Come on," he coaxed. "Give me a chance to prove I'm not the same old Brian anymore. I've matured, like a bottle of fine wine."

"Sure." Enid giggled. "Where have you been, in a wine cellar?"

"No, Colorado," Brian said. "On top of the Rockies, where everything is clear. I'm telling you, I really have changed."

Enid bit her lip. Maybe he was telling the truth. One thing was certain: Brian was very flattering and very charming. And Enid was grateful for the attention. At least there was one person who was interested in her. He was very good-looking, too, and he was in college. Maybe it was time to give Brian Saunders the benefit of the doubt. After all, not only had *she* changed, but her former boyfriend, George Warren, had been part of the same crowd, and he was a totally different person now.

"So what's it going to be?" he pressed. "Give me a chance?"

"OK, OK." Enid laughed. "If it will shut you up, I'll go out to dinner with you."

There was silence at the other end. "Brian?" she asked.

"I thought you wanted me to shut up," he teased.

Enid smiled. She was beginning to feel a little better about life. It would be a nice surprise if Brian was the one to turn things around for her.

"Just kidding," she said. "I'll see you later."

"Great. I'll pick you up at eight-thirty. I can't wait."

Enid hung up the phone and smiled. Well, she thought, at least she couldn't complain that Christmas vacation had been boring so far! And if Brian had changed as much as he said he

had, then her vacation could be taking a defi-
nite turn for the better.

There's only one way to find out, she decided.

She went upstairs to take a shower and get
ready for her evening.

Eight

Enid was ready by the time Brian pulled up in front of her house. She ran down the stairs and out the front door. He was walking up to the house, and they met halfway.

"Hi. You look so nice." Brian gave her an appreciative look.

Enid felt a small tingle of happiness. "Thanks," she murmured.

Brian had complimented her right away. That afternoon, Jeffrey had never even noticed her appearance. Maybe it made sense not to chase after someone whose mind was somewhere else. Brian was here and he appreciated her, and that made a big difference. Enid began to do some serious reevaluating. Yes, it was best to stop thinking about Jeffrey and to start concentrating on Brian.

"Where are we going?" she asked as she got into his car.

Brian gave her a mischievous smile. "It's a surprise." Then he laughed. "Actually, I'm no good at surprises. We're going to a Thai restaurant. I eat a lot of Thai food at school, and I thought you might enjoy it."

"Thai food?" Enid repeated. She had no idea what it would be like, but it certainly sounded exotic.

"You'll love it," Brian promised. "But it's pretty spicy. Just a warning."

Enid grinned. "I think I can handle it. My mother makes the hottest chili north of the Mexican border. I'm used to spicy food!"

"OK. But don't say I didn't warn you." Driving through Sweet Valley, Brian seemed relaxed and confident, nothing like the old hell-raiser Enid used to know.

"So, what brought about this amazing change in you?" Enid finally asked.

"Was I that bad?" Brian responded, smiling ruefully.

"Sorry." Enid laughed. "You really were, though. But I'm serious. What changed you?"

Brian frowned for a moment while he negoti-ated the traffic. "Well, I guess going away to college did it. I function a lot better in a more independent environment than I did in high school, where it was like being in the army. And I'm taking a lot of classes in Asian studies."

"No wonder you like Thai food!"

"Right," Brian agreed. "Eastern philosophy has really straightened out my head. It's amazing."

Enid was surprised at how different Brian seemed. He was charming and interesting. And he was certainly a lot more sophisticated than the boys she knew at school. Her pulse raced as he gave her another admiring glance.

"Here it is," Brian said as they pulled into the parking lot of the Bangkok Palace.

He took her hand as they walked into the restaurant. The interior was dim and mysteri-ous, and carved wooden screens created tiny private dining nooks. A waiter showed them to a table for two and left them with the menus.

"I don't know what any of these dishes are," Enid said after glancing at the menu. "I don't even know how to pronounce them!"

Brian smiled. "I'll order for both of us, OK?"

"Sure."

Enid glanced around and noticed two college-age girls looking at Brian and whispering. Enid felt a rush of pleasure. She was out with a very good-looking guy! Her unhappiness and worry about her parents, Jeffrey, and Elizabeth began to fade.

"Tell me more about college," she said after the waiter had taken their order.

"You *have* to go to Colorado, Enid," Brian said. "It's so fantastic. The mountains are incredible. Once you've been in the Rockies, your whole life suddenly makes sense." Brian smiled bashfully. "I'm not explaining myself very well."

"No, go on," Enid said, touched by his enthusiasm. "I'm really interested."

While Brian spoke, Enid found herself comparing him to Jeffrey. She still felt a twinge of regret, but she told herself firmly that Brian was making up for it. Jeffrey was a nice boy, but Brian was so much more mature and knowledgeable. He was grown-up, and Jeffrey was still a kid in many ways. Maybe it really had all worked out for the best.

"Here's our dinner," Brian announced, looking over her shoulder.

The waiter set several steaming plates of food on the table. Enid breathed in the sweet and spicy aromas. She could identify shrimp, peanuts, red peppers, noodles, bean sprouts, and cucumbers on the dishes spread out before them.

"It smells great," she said, helping herself.

"Do you want a beer?" Brian asked. "You need something cool to drink with this food."

"I'll stick with water," she replied.

"You don't mind if I have one?"

"Of course not." Enid knew that it was possible to drink beer sensibly. And beer was probably refreshing with spicy food.

Throughout their meal Enid and Brian talked easily about a lot of things. Brian told her more about his Asian studies classes, and Enid told him about her friends at Sweet Valley High and about how she was looking forward to seeing her father the next day. Between them they finished all the food, including two dishes of pineapple ice cream for dessert.

"Thanks," Enid told him as they left the restaurant. "That was really great."

Brian looked down at her and gave her a smile that made her bones turn to water. "You're welcome."

Enid wondered if Brian was going to suggest they go somewhere to be alone for a while. She debated with herself whether she wanted to do that yet, or whether that would be rushing things. She felt a nervous tingle of anticipation.

"Do you have to go right home?" he asked as he started the car.

"Oh, um . . ." Enid blushed and looked out the window. She didn't know what to say.

"If you want, we could stop by and see some friends of mine," Brian said. "I told them that we might come by to say hello."

"Is it a party?" Enid asked hesitantly. It wasn't that she didn't like parties; it was that when she had known Brian before, they had both been at some pretty wild parties.

"No—nothing organized or anything," he assured her. "It's just different people home from college for the Christmas break. Old friends getting together. That's all."

Brian reached over and squeezed Enid's hand. "Come on. You'll like them. We don't have to stay very long. Then I'll take you home."

"OK," Enid agreed, returning his smile.

"Good." Brian stepped on the gas, and they headed across town.

For a moment Enid wondered if she had made a mistake. Now that she had agreed to go with Brian, he seemed more intent on getting there than on talking to her. Each time she tried to start a conversation, he answered in monosyllables. And he was driving pretty fast, too. *He's just eager to see his friends*, Enid told herself. *And he* does *want them to meet me.* That was flattering.

"This is it," Brian said. Cars were double-parked on both sides of the street. "I guess a few people showed up."

"A few," Enid said wryly.

Brian parked almost a block away from the house. They could hear the music as they walked back. "This looks like a party to me." Enid said. She stopped on the sidewalk and stared at the house. She could see a crowd of people silhouetted against the windows.

"Yeah, well, I guess it turned into one," Brian said sheepishly. He took her hand. "Come on. Let's go in and say hello."

A blast of music greeted them as the door opened. The people inside were packed in like sardines. Smoke and laughter filled the air.

"Brian!" voices called out. "Merry Christmas!"

"How are you?" he shouted to a girl right next to them. "This is Enid! Enid, this is Jackie!"

Enid smiled politely, but Jackie was already deep in conversation with Brian. Enid looked around. She saw a few people from her old crowd, and she turned away, hoping they wouldn't remember or recognize her. She also saw beer bottles, overflowing ashtrays, and joints being passed from hand to hand. She began to feel sick. Coming here had been a big mistake.

"Brian?"

But Brian wasn't standing beside her anymore.

"Here!" Someone jostled Enid's elbow and shoved a brimming plastic cup of beer in her hand.

"I don't—" Enid started to say, but the boy who handed it to her had already melted into the crowd. Frowning, Enid put the beer down on a table.

The music was so loud, it hurt her ears, and the air was dense with smoke. Enid recognized the familiar sweet scent of pot, something she hadn't smelled in a very long time. She had to get some fresh air before it started going to her head.

"Have you seen Brian Saunders?" she shouted to a girl next to her.

"I think he's in the kitchen!" the girl yelled back.

"Where's the kitchen?" Enid asked. But the girl didn't bother to answer.

Enid felt more and more angry. She scanned the crowd anxiously and then felt a jolt of surprise. She recognized several more people from her old partying days. Back then, when she was usually drunk or stoned, they had all seemed so funny and so cool. Now, watching them swilling beer, Enid thought they looked like losers.

Fighting back mild panic, Enid made her way through the crowd to the back of the house. In the kitchen a very drunk girl was laughing with long, high-pitched gasps. Three guys were passing around a bottle of bourbon.

"Have you seen Brian Saunders?" Enid asked them. She was embarrassed for the girl, who was now hanging on the arm of one of the boys and whispering in his ear.

"Downstairs," one of the boys said, gesturing broadly with the bottle. "At the bar."

Enid felt her stomach sink. It was no use pretending anymore that Brian was there just to hang out with his friends. Enid made her way carefully down the stairs, stepping around several couples who seemed completely unaware of her.

A big crowd filled the furnished basement. A noisy group of guys was clustered at one end of a bar that ran the entire length of the wall. Brian was with them.

On the bar sat a big cup of beer covered with a piece of paper toweling held in place by a rubber band. In the center sat a quarter. The guys were taking turns burning holes in the paper with a cigarette lighter and matches.

"Look out, Saunders." Someone laughed. "Try to finesse this one."

Laughing, Brian lit a match and held it to the paper. The paper flared.

"Brian," Enid said, touching his elbow.

101

He didn't seem to hear her. A chorus of cheers went up as the paper burned through and the quarter fell into the cup of beer.

"Chug! Chug! Chug!"

"Brian!" Enid begged.

"Hang on," he said laughing.

Enid realized that Brian was already drunk. He hadn't changed at all. While she watched, he started chugging the beer. Finally he slammed the cup down, took the quarter out of his mouth, and placed it on the bar. The other guys started to cheer.

"Brian?" Enid said again.

He turned and noticed her for the first time. "Oh, Enid," he said, smiling guiltily. "Do you know the guys? These are the guys," he said with a grand sweep of his hand, knocking over two cups of beer in the process.

"I'd like to leave now."

"But we just got here." Brian's breath was rank with beer. "Where's your holiday spirit?"

Disgusted, Enid turned and walked away. She couldn't trust Brian to drive in his condition. When she got upstairs, she found a quiet room and called a cab company. Then she fought her way out through the crowd and stood on the corner to wait for the taxi.

By the time she got home, Enid's spirits had sunk to an all-time low. She knew that she could forget about ever seeing Brian again. All of his impressive talk about the Rocky Mountains and Eastern philosophy straightening him out was just a lot of bull. He was still the same old Brian, too weak to turn down a drink or to resist a chance to party. There was nothing there for her. Nothing at all.

And there was nothing to replace losing Jeffrey, even though she had never really had him in the first place. All of the disappointment she had felt earlier in the day came flooding back.

She desperately needed someone to talk to, but there was no one. She wished her father would call.

Tired and sad, Enid sat down in the living room and stared at the Christmas tree. When she was little, she had thought that the family Christmas tree was the most magical thing in the world. Just thinking about it had been enough to fill her with joy and excitement.

Now looking at the tree reminded her of how empty her world had become.

The sooner the holiday was over, the better. So far, it had brought her nothing but disappointment and unhappiness.

"Merry Christmas," she said out loud.

Then she slowly climbed the stairs and went to bed.

Nine

Elizabeth woke up early the morning of Christmas Eve. The house was quiet. Everyone else was still asleep. Prince Albert, the family's golden Labrador retriever, greeted her as she walked into the kitchen.

"Hey, Prince," Elizabeth said softly, stroking his head. "You'll get walked soon." She sat down at the kitchen table and stared into space.

What am I doing? she wondered.

In retrospect, Elizabeth couldn't believe that she had baked cookies for Jeffrey and taken them to his house. What if somebody found out? What if *Todd* found out? She would never be able to explain it; she couldn't even explain it to herself.

Luckily, Lila had temporarily moved in with the Wakefields to spend Christmas with them. And that meant that Jessica was distracted. Neither she nor Lila had even asked who Elizabeth had been baking for.

Elizabeth stared at the telephone for a while. She wished she could talk to someone about what she had done. Talking might help make her motives clearer to herself. But considering what she had said to Enid about Jeffrey at the skating rink, she knew she couldn't discuss the situation with her best friend. Calling Enid the previous morning had been a mistake. She knew she had made a fool of herself, both at the rink and at Jeffrey's house, but she just hadn't known how to explain her feelings to Enid.

As she continued to gaze absently at the phone, it rang. Elizabeth jumped up to answer it before it woke anyone up.

"Hello?" she said softly.

"Liz? It's me."

Elizabeth let out a gasp of surprise and relief. "Todd! I'm so glad you called!"

"I didn't wake you up, did I?" he asked. "I know that it's later out here, but I couldn't wait any longer to call you."

Smiling, Elizabeth wrapped the phone cord around her finger and sat back down at the table. "Why?" she asked, although she knew the answer.

"Because I miss you," he said tenderly. "I wish we could be together on Christmas Eve."

"Me, too." Elizabeth sighed. "Are you having fun skiing?"

"It's fantastic!" he said enthusiastically. "There's only one thing missing here. You."

"Did you open my present yet?" Elizabeth asked.

"No way! Christmas morning, and not before." Todd laughed. "Listen, I have an idea. Tonight, before you go to bed, look up at the Big Dipper. I'll do it, too. That way, it'll be like we're together."

Elizabeth's heart overflowed with love for him. "I will. Oh, Todd, I love you."

"I love you, too," he said softly. "I have to go. But I'll call you Christmas day, OK?"

"Great!" Elizabeth said. "Talk to you then." As she hung up the phone, Elizabeth let out a dreamy sigh. *Nobody* made her feel the way Todd did. There was no doubt in her mind about her feelings for him.

Elizabeth was still lost in her daydreams when

Jessica and Lila walked into the kitchen, still in their pajamas.

"Did you make coffee?" Jessica asked in a creaky, sleepy voice.

"No." Elizabeth sighed and smiled happily.

"Did you bring in the paper?"

Elizabeth put her chin in her hands. "No," she said in a dreamy voice.

Jessica and Lila exchanged a meaningful look. "Did Todd call?" Jessica asked.

"Yes."

"No wonder," Lila said. "There's only one thing that could explain that glazed look."

Jessica laughed. "Right. True love."

"Actually, being whacked on the head might produce the same effect," Lila retorted.

Grinning, Elizabeth stood up and retied her bathrobe. "In my case, it's true love. Now, if you'll excuse me . . ."

Even with Todd gone for the holidays, Elizabeth felt closer to him than ever. No matter what else happened, she knew she would always love him.

Enid woke up on Christmas Eve morning with a pounding headache. She lay on her bed, staring at the ceiling and remembering what a fi-

108

asco her date with Brian had been. Groaning, she rolled over and buried her head under her pillow. She wished that she could stay in bed forever.

Suddenly Enid let out a gasp and sat bolt upright.

"Dad!"

She flung back the covers and scrambled out of bed. Today was the day she would finally see her father after so many months. The thought of waiting until lunchtime made her wild with impatience.

"What am I going to wear?" she wondered out loud and threw open her closet door. Distractedly, she yanked blouses and sweaters off their hangers and tossed them onto the bed.

"Mom?" Enid yelled. "Can I borrow that green sweater of yours?"

"Sure," her mother called back from downstairs. "It's in my closet."

Enid ran to her mother's room. On the bureau was a picture of Enid and her father, taken at her fourth birthday party. Mr. Rollins was carrying her on his shoulders, and a party hat was perched on her head. It was the only picture of Mr. Rollins in the house, except for the ones Enid had in her room. Enid guessed that her mother had kept it only because Enid herself looked so happy.

"Hi, Dad," Enid whispered to the photo. She kissed her fingertip and pressed it to his face.

"You look nice," Mrs. Rollins said when Enid walked into the kitchen. "Did you have fun last night?"

Enid rolled her eyes. "I'd prefer not to talk about it," she said. "I thought that Brian Saunders was a new person, but people never change."

"You did," her mother said and smiled.

Enid smiled back. "Well, OK. But Brian never will."

"Sometimes it take something pretty drastic to make a person realize that what they're doing is destructive," Mrs. Rollins pointed out. "It did for you."

"I know." Enid poured herself some orange juice, then took a sip of it. She was too excited about seeing her father to talk about Brian. "I'm leaving right after breakfast," she announced.

"I thought your father wasn't expecting you until noon."

"He's not," Enid agreed. "But I'm going to surprise him and get there a little early. Besides, I have some errands to run first. I want to get him a present. I should get to the hotel by about eleven-thirty."

After a quick meal, Enid ran upstairs to check her appearance one more time. She wanted to look special for her father. She was happy with what she saw in the mirror. She knew her father would kiss her and call her his little princess. It might be childish, but she didn't care.

Enid did her last-minute shopping quickly, and at a quarter to twelve she pulled into the parking lot at the Sweet Valley Regency. Her heart was pounding with anticipation as she ran up the steps.

"Hello. What room is Mr. Rollins in?" Enid asked the desk clerk.

The woman checked her register. "Number five-fourteen, but he left a message saying he'd be in the Oak Room. Are you his daughter?"

Enid nodded quickly. "Yes. Where is it?" The clerk pointed down the hallway, and Enid hurried off in that direction.

The Oak Room was an elegant wood-paneled restaurant with leather chairs and dark green tablecloths. Enid was proud that her father wanted to treat her to lunch at such a fancy place. The headwaiter met her at the door.

"I'm supposed to meet my father here," Enid

said before the man had a chance to speak. "Mr. Rollins?"

"Mr. Rollins is at the bar," the waiter said.

Grinning from ear to ear, Enid headed for the back of the Oak Room, where a glittering row of bottles marked the bar. She spotted her father. He had his back to her, and she went up to him and put her hands over his eyes.

"Guess who?" She laughed.

Mr. Rollins turned around awkwardly, a big smile lighting his face. "Honey! Enid!" He lurched to one side and nearly fell off the bar stool. "How's my little princess?"

Enid stared at him, her smile fading. There was an empty glass on the bar in front of him, and she could smell gin on his breath.

"Daddy?" she asked in a puzzled voice. Her eyes went to his glass and then back to him.

"Just had a couple of drinks," her father said hastily.

"A couple?" Enid repeated. "Daddy, you're drunk, aren't you?"

"Drunk?" Mr. Rollins looked over at the bartender and forced a laugh. "Is that any way to talk to your father, young lady?"

Enid was shocked and hurt. She could not believe that her father was drunk before twelve o'clock, and on the day they were seeing each

112

other for the first time in months! It was horrible. He was having real trouble staying on the bar stool, and his speech was slurred. There was no question about it. He was trashed.

"I'm sorry, sweetie," Mr. Rollins went on contritely. "I've been on the wagon a long time. Honest. I only meant to have one."

Enid stood motionless.

"But I got to thinking about how I upset your mother every time I come around, about how I always let you down, and about how I've missed seeing you grow up. I just needed a little pick-me-up." He tried to square his shoulders manfully, and then he gestured to the bartender.

"Dad!" Enid gasped.

"Just soda water this time," he said to the bartender. Then he turned to Enid. "You're grown up now, Enid. You should know that there's nothing wrong with having a couple. Besides, I remember you used to do a little drinking yourself."

A roaring sound filled Enid's ears. Tears welled up in her eyes as she turned and stumbled away.

"Enid!" Mr. Rollins called. "Wait—don't go! I'm sorry—"

Blinded by tears, Enid ran through the hotel lobby and out to the parking lot. She was so upset that she felt sick to her stomach.

What could have made him get drunk today of all days? she asked herself in anguish. He had mentioned feeling bad about upsetting her mother. That had to be it, Enid decided. And the more she thought about it, the more convinced she was that it was all her mother's fault. If only she wasn't so nasty to him every time he called, this never would have happened.

By the time she got home, Enid was furious with her mother.

"Enid? What are you doing home?" Mrs. Rollins asked in surprise. She was sitting in the living room, writing some last-minute Christmas cards.

"You really did it this time, Mom," Enid fumed. "You've been so mean to Dad lately that he went and got drunk. And it's all because of you."

Mrs. Rollins looked very sad. "Your father was drunk when you got to the hotel?"

"Yes. And it's all your fault!" Fresh tears rolled down Enid's face.

"Enid," her mother said sharply, "look at me. There's only one person responsible for your father's drinking—your father."

"No! You're the one who made him so upset that he lost his confidence," Enid retorted.

Mrs. Rollins shook her head. "Don't you understand? It doesn't matter what I say to him or how I act. *He's* the one pouring the gin down his throat, not me."

Enid felt her anger crumbling away, leaving nothing but pain and emptiness in its place. She couldn't get the devastating picture of her father nearly falling off the bar stool out of her mind. She sat down on the couch, trying to control her tears. "Why is this happening?" she sobbed.

"Oh, honey." Mrs. Rollins sat down next to Enid on the couch and put her arms around her. "Your father has a real drinking problem, and it has nothing to do with you or me or anyone else. I tried for a long time to help him stop, but it didn't work. He's the only one who can make a change in his life."

"But why *doesn't* he?" Enid sniffed. "Why couldn't I be important enough for him not to drink today?"

Her mother hugged her tight. "I don't know, Enid. I know that he loves you, but he's also dependent on alcohol."

"Couldn't *I* make him change?" Enid pleaded.

"No. The desire to change has to come from him," her mother said firmly. "I told you before, Enid, sometimes it takes something drastic to make a person want to change. Maybe he just hasn't hit a crisis point yet."

Though she knew that what her mother was saying was true, Enid didn't want to listen. Her father didn't love her enough to stop drinking, she didn't have a boyfriend, and she could not even talk to her best friend anymore. This was the worst Christmas of her entire life.

Enid wiped her nose and sat up. The look on her mother's face was one of sympathy, but it didn't make Enid feel any better.

"I always tried to help him, sweetheart," Mrs. Rollins said. "But finally, I had to make a decision. I could sacrifice you and myself to him and his problems, or I could take you away and try to start over. He's on his own now."

"It's just not right," Enid said. She felt tired and hopeless.

As they sat there, each thinking her own thoughts, the telephone rang. Enid covered her face with her hands and groaned.

"I'll get it," her mother said and went into the kitchen.

Enid heard her mother say, "Hi, Jeffrey."

In a panic, Enid stood up and ran to her mother's side. She wanted her to tell Jeffrey that she wasn't home. But Mrs. Rollins handed her the phone.

Sighing, Enid took the receiver. If nothing else, Jeffrey was a friend. And Enid needed a friend right now.

"Hi," she said gloomily.

"Hey, Sonja. You sound like you're getting a cold," Jeffrey said, concerned. "Are you all right?"

Enid debated quickly. If she said that she was sick, she could get out of having to do anything. But she couldn't bear the thought of being by herself any longer.

"No, I'm OK," she said. "What's up?"

"I just wanted to see if you had decided about going to the party tonight." There was a long pause. "Well? Are you going?"

Enid shrugged. "I guess so."

"How about if I pick you up, then?" he went on. "About seven-thirty?"

"OK," she agreed after a moment's pause. "I'll see you later."

Ten

After the Wakefields' traditional Christmas Eve dinner, Elizabeth, Jessica, and Lila crowded into the twins' two-seater convertible. They weren't planning to stay long at George and Robin's party, just long enough to wish all their friends happy holidays one more time. Then they would head back home to spend the rest of the evening with the family, including the twins' brother, Steven, who had come home from the state university earlier that day.

"Why do I always get stuck with you sitting on my lap, Fowler?" Jessica grumbled. "You're totally destroying my outfit."

"Better yours than mine," Lila responded.

"You could always sit in the back," Jessica pointed out. The Fiat Spider didn't have a back seat, but there was a small space where it was possible for a person to sit sideways.

"With all that stuff you throw back there? No way!"

Elizabeth laughed and put the car into gear. "It's Christmas Eve! Can't you guys stop picking on each other?"

Lila and Jessica both stared at her. "Why would we do that?"

"Just a dumb idea I had," Elizabeth said, laughing. "I guess the spirit of Christmas doesn't stand a chance with you two around."

"Just drive, Liz," Jessica commanded in a lofty tone. "We have a party to attend."

When they arrived at George Warren's house, the three girls were immediately engulfed in a sea of friends. It seemed as if the entire junior and senior classes from Sweet Valley High were there, as well as friends who had graduated and gone on to college. Steven was already there with his girlfriend, Cara Walker.

"Merry Christmas!" Elizabeth yelled, giving Cara a hug.

"Same to you," Cara shouted back. A cheer went up across the room as someone opened a gift.

After taking a cup of eggnog, Elizabeth looked appreciatively around the room. The Warrens' house was warm and cozy and smelled like spruce and cinnamon.

Elizabeth caught sight of Enid standing alone in a doorway. She knew that it was time to make amends for the silly way she had acted. She grabbed another cup of eggnog and wove through the crowd to her friend. "Merry Christmas," she said softly, giving Enid a kiss on the cheek.

"Oh, hi, Liz," Enid replied. "Merry Christmas."

Enid seemed anything but merry. Her green eyes were downcast, and a small frown creased her forehead.

"What's wrong?" Elizabeth asked. "You look upset."

Enid shrugged and took a sip of her eggnog. She wouldn't meet her friend's eyes. "Oh, nothing. I get this way sometimes around the holidays."

"Did you see your father?" Elizabeth asked.

Enid's eyes filled with tears. She put one hand up to her face in embarrassment and turned away.

"Enid! What is it?" Elizabeth asked. "What's wrong?"

"It's nothing, really," Enid said, sniffing and giving Elizabeth an overly bright smile. "It didn't work out, but that's OK. So, this is a pretty great party, isn't it?"

Elizabeth frowned. Something was very wrong, and it worried her that Enid didn't want to talk about it. "Do you want to go somewhere quiet and tell me what happened?"

"No!" Enid tried to laugh, but she still couldn't meet Elizabeth's eyes. "Oh, there's Dana. I wanted to ask her something. I'll see you later, OK?"

Before Elizabeth could object, Enid hurried away. Elizabeth shook her head. It made her sad to see her friend so upset on Christmas Eve.

"Merry Christmas," said a voice in her ear.

Elizabeth looked up to see Jeffrey standing beside her. "Jeffrey! Listen, I wanted to—"

"I think we should—"

They both stopped and laughed at their own awkwardness. Jeffrey gestured toward the back of the house. "Can I talk to you for a minute?"

"Sure," Elizabeth said. She realized that there were still some things left unsaid between them and that it was best to get them out in the open. She followed him down a hallway and into the quiet book-lined den. The noise of the party faded behind them as Jeffrey closed the door.

Once they were alone, neither one of them knew how to begin. Elizabeth bit her lip, searching for the right words. She knew that she had confused her feelings of loneliness with still caring for Jeffrey, but she wasn't sure how to explain herself. Jeffrey was pacing back and forth.

"Liz, when you came over yesterday . . ." he began.

"Wait!" Elizabeth pleaded. "Before you say anything, I just want to tell you that I still care a lot about you, Jeffrey. But I really love Todd, and I know I don't have any claim on you anymore."

Jeffrey looked at her and smiled painfully. "I know. The other day I thought that there was still a chance for us. But that's crazy. I know it's over between us, Liz, but I'll always think of you as a very special person."

"When I brought you the cookies, I didn't mean to hurt you," Elizabeth said. She sat down on the edge of the sofa and tried to collect her thoughts. "Maybe deep down, I wanted you to still be in love with me, but that's not fair. I want you to be as happy as I am. I really mean that."

Jeffrey's emotions showed clearly in his eyes, and Elizabeth had to look away. It hurt not to be in love with him anymore. He was a special person.

"I can be. I will be," Jeffrey said at last. "I've been telling myself—well, forget it."

"You're great, Jeffrey," Elizabeth said warmly. "I hope we can always be really good friends. And I'm not just saying that."

"I know. You always mean what you say," he agreed. "I told Enid—" He broke off, suddenly looking very shy.

Elizabeth felt a flicker of surprise. "You've been spending a lot of time with Enid lately, haven't you?"

"Well, I guess I have," he admitted.

"Do you like her? You know what I mean," Elizabeth added.

"I think I do," Jeffrey said slowly. "I always thought of her as just a friend, but lately . . ."

"She's a wonderful person, Jeffrey."

"I know," he said.

"I think that you should trust your feelings." Elizabeth put her hand on his arm. "If there's a chance for you two . . ."

Jeffrey nodded. "I don't know. I've been really confused lately. But I know that I've got to talk to her tonight, if it's possible."

Elizabeth stood up. "I'm really glad we cleared things up."

"Me, too. Now, let's get back to the party, OK? People are going to start talking."

"And that's the last thing we need!" Elizabeth led the way back down the hallway. As they reentered the living room Jeffrey touched her arm. She looked back at him and saw that he was pointing toward the ceiling. Over their heads was a sprig of mistletoe.

"Well?" Jeffrey said, his eyes dancing.

"Merry Christmas!" Elizabeth stood on tiptoe to kiss him. Their lips met, and Elizabeth realized that there was no lingering magic. It was truly over between them. She was glad, but it made her a little wistful, too.

"Merry Christmas, Liz," Jeffrey said in a low and tender voice.

Elizabeth looked up at him with a full heart and impulsively gave him a hug. She knew now that they would always be friends.

From across the room, Enid saw Elizabeth and Jeffrey kiss, and her heart plunged.

I don't believe it, she thought. *Here we go again.*

Even though Jeffrey had asked her to the party, picked her up, and told her he was glad to see her, there he was kissing Elizabeth again. Enid felt numb.

I can't win, she told herself. *I just can't win*. Coming to the party had been a huge mistake. It was obvious that Jeffrey would *never* get over Elizabeth. Especially now that Elizabeth was so obviously leading him on.

Fighting back tears, Enid pushed her way through the crowd and out to the patio. She sank into a chair and tipped her head back. She felt more alone than ever. The distant noises of the party only intensified her feeling of isolation.

Why do I even try? she wondered. *What was the point of going straight and pulling myself together if this is where it gets me? At least before, I was too stoned to notice how miserable life can be.*

As Enid sat by herself, gazing forlornly at the stars, a tear trickled down her cheek. The rest of the world was celebrating, and she had never been so unhappy in her life.

Jessica moved among the dancers, eagerly scanning the crowd. What she wanted was someone new to flirt with. Every face in the room was so boringly familiar, she wanted to scream.

Then she saw Brian Saunders.

Hello, hello, hello, she said silently and smiled.

It was typical of Enid to be so negative about Brian, Jessica thought. Enid claimed not to be interested in him, but what other reason could she have for trying to warn Jessica away from him? Jealousy, plain and simple.

But all's fair in love and war, she added.

Besides, Brian couldn't possibly be interested in Enid. Or he wouldn't be once he got to know Jessica. Compared to her, Enid was bland and boring. Jessica was confident that she could win Brian over before the party broke up.

"Jess, do you want to dance?" George Warren asked her.

She smiled at him. At any other time, she would have been happy to flirt with Robin's boyfriend. But right now she had her sights set on Brian Saunders.

"Sorry, George," she said. "I wish I could, but there's someone I have to talk to."

"OK. See you later," George replied easily.

Jessica smoothed her royal blue minidress over her hips and moistened her lips with her tongue. Then she tossed her hair back and crossed the room.

"Hi, Brian," she said, walking up behind him. "Remember me?"

Brian looked at her blankly for a moment and then smiled. "Oh, right. Jennifer?"

"Jessica," she corrected him. She gave him a dazzling smile. "I didn't know you were going to be here."

"George is an old friend of mine," Brian said, looking around the room distractedly.

"I guess we have something in common, then," Jessica replied.

"What? Oh, right. Say, you know Enid Rollins, too, right?"

Jessica's sweet expression hardened. "Yes."

"Is she here tonight?" Brian asked hopefully.

"Yes," Jessica said in an icy tone. He wasn't exactly falling at her feet with adoration. It was time to turn the charm up a few notches. "Listen, Brian, would you like to—"

"Where is she, do you know?"

Jessica glared at him. "I haven't the faintest idea," she said coldly. Then she turned on her heel and stalked away.

"Ooooh, I could just—just bite someone," she growled at Lila.

Lila popped a walnut in her mouth and raised her eyebrows languidly. "That sounds like fun. Did you have anyone particular in mind?"

"You have a dirty mind, Fowler," Jessica said and walked off.

"Jessica!"

She whirled around at the sound of a boy calling her name. She was pleasantly surprised to see Jeffrey coming toward her.

"Hey, French," she said, giving him a playful grin. "How's it go—"

"Have you seen Enid anywhere?" Jeffrey interrupted.

"No," she replied curtly.

Jessica watched in amazement as Jeffrey strode past her without stopping.

"What is going on here?" she muttered. And then she saw her twin. "Liz! Finally, someone who likes me."

"What are you talking about?" Elizabeth asked. "Listen, have you seen Enid around?"

Jessica clapped both hands over her ears. "I don't believe this!"

"What's wrong?" Elizabeth asked, looking over her shoulder as she spoke.

"Forget it," Jessica said. "Just tell me this: What did Enid do that made her so popular all of a sudden?"

Elizabeth frowned. "Nothing. I just wanted to talk to her."

"You and half the world," Jessica said. "No, I

haven't seen her. Just follow the crowd, they're all looking for her, too," she said, waving her hand.

Elizabeth shrugged. "I'm sure there's a logical explanation for the way you're behaving, but you can tell me later."

"Yeah, right." Jessica slumped onto the couch. Something was up with Enid, but Jessica wasn't sufficiently interested to pursue this mystery.

Sighing, she looked around the room one more time and spotted her brother talking to a cute guy. Jessica's eyebrows went up. Fresh possibilities loomed on the horizon. The evening might not be a total waste, Jessica mused as she stood and crossed the room toward them.

Eleven

Heaving a weary sigh, Enid stood up and headed back to the party. She had decided to leave as soon as she could find a ride. Obviously, she wasn't going to ask Jeffrey to take her home. He would want to stay and be with Elizabeth for as long as possible. Enid wanted to kick herself for having gotten her hopes up again.

You'll never learn, she scolded herself. *You're such a fool.*

She walked back into the living room. The first person she saw was Brian Saunders. Startled, she quickly turned to slip out to the patio again.

131

"Enid!" Brian called, immediately crossing the room.

Enid looked around in a panic. She didn't want to talk to him, but she couldn't just run away. Feeling trapped, she stood and waited for him to reach her. She would tell him straight off that she despised him.

"Am I glad I found you!" he exclaimed.

Enid gave him a frigid look. "I'm not."

"Listen, I want to apologize for last night, Enid. I can't believe I did that. I'm really embarrassed."

"You should be," Enid said coolly. But she was thrown a little bit off balance. She had expected him to be defensive and act as if his getting drunk didn't matter. Instead, he was apologizing.

"You know how it is," he went on. "When you get with old friends who are used to you being a certain way, they expect you to still be that way."

"So you always do what your friends expect you to do?"

"No, that's not what I meant," he said quickly. "It's just that old habits are hard to break. I'm not saying that as an excuse. That's just the truth."

It sounded like an excuse to Enid, but she didn't comment. She was curious to hear what else he was going to say.

Brian fidgeted with the cup in his hands. "I know I'll never be able to impress a girl like you if I can't get my act together. What can I say? I have a weak character." He gave her a boyish, coaxing smile. "I'm trying my best."

In spite of herself, Enid smiled back. "You sure do have a weak character."

"Give me another chance to show you I've really changed," Brian pleaded as he took a step closer. "Wouldn't you like to reform me? It would be an act of mercy."

Enid looked up at him and tried to keep her wits together. Everything he said was so flattering that she didn't really know what to think. If Brian was really trying to straighten out because of her, that was important, wasn't it?

Still, he had used practically the same line the other night and had gone ahead and gotten drunk anyway.

"I think the biggest act of mercy would be to have you humanely destroyed," Enid said dryly. "I know a good vet who could put you out of your misery."

"Enid, I'm crushed," he replied in a low, seductive voice. His smile was incredibly sexy. "Don't you know I'm making a heroic effort here?"

"Yeah, right." Enid rolled her eyes. He was making a heroic effort at something, but she doubted that it was at straightening out.

Enid had just decided to walk away from him when she saw Elizabeth heading in her direction. From Elizabeth's earnest expression, Enid suspected that her friend wanted to talk to her about something important. For a moment, Enid felt relieved to have someone rescue her from the clutches of the relentless Brian. But then she remembered seeing Elizabeth and Jeffrey kiss under the mistletoe.

"You're just too much," she said to Brian with an unmistakably flirtatious smile. "You know that, don't you?"

"Enid?" Elizabeth broke in.

"We need more privacy," Brian whispered in Enid's ear.

"Can I talk to you for a second?" Elizabeth asked.

"Sorry, I'm kind of tied up right now, Liz," Enid explained as she turned her back on her friend.

"It's important, though." Elizabeth met Enid's gaze and widened her eyes as though to say, *What's going on?*

Enid sighed impatiently. "I'll talk to you later, OK, Liz?"

Baffled, Elizabeth looked from Enid to Brian. "OK," she said, and she walked away.

"I didn't want any interruptions," Enid explained to Brian, loud enough for Elizabeth to hear.

Enid hoped that Elizabeth had gotten her message loud and clear. It was only fair that she get some attention for a while, and she wanted Elizabeth to know what it felt like to be snubbed.

"Let's dance," Enid suggested.

Just as she spoke, someone put a new tape on the recorder. The first song was slow and romantic. Brian held her very, very close as they began to dance. Enid rested her cheek against his chest and tried to enjoy herself. Brian's arms moved down her back, and she shrugged uncomfortably.

"Enid?"

She opened her eyes. Jeffrey was standing beside them.

"Enid's dancing with me," Brian said firmly.

"Can I talk to you when this song is over?" Jeffrey asked, ignoring Brian.

Enid felt a wave of resentment wash over her. Jeffrey probably just wanted to ask her about Elizabeth. The only reason he liked her was because she was friends with Elizabeth. But he had come to the wrong place for advice.

You can just forget it, she told him silently. She closed her eyes and wrapped her arms more tightly around Brian's neck.

"Enid?" Jeffrey asked again.

"We're busy right now," Brian said warningly.

Enid opened her eyes again and gave Jeffrey a sweet smile. "Liz is over there, talking to Steve and Cara," she said politely.

"Huh?" Jeffrey looked puzzled and shook his head. "No, I wanted to—"

"Right over there," Enid said, pointing. "Sitting on the couch."

Jeffrey frowned. "But, Enid—"

"Bye, Jeffrey," Enid said, letting Brian steer her away.

"You don't want to talk to anyone but me?" Brian whispered in her ear.

Enid nodded against his shoulder. "Mmm. That's right."

"Good," Brian said, holding her even closer. "That's the way it should be."

Enid thought of the confused look on Jeffrey's face, and she was pleased. She was tired of being a counselor for Elizabeth and Jeffrey's romance. He was on his own as far as Enid was concerned. It was her turn to have a good time and she wasn't going to let anything interfere with that.

"You're a great dancer," Brian said.

Enid looked up at him and felt a tingle of happiness. He was smiling at her with undisguised admiration. "You're not so bad yourself," she teased.

He grinned. "No, I'm not."

In fact, Enid liked him more each minute. He was very good-looking, a great dancer, and he obviously liked her. One little slipup wasn't exactly a federal crime, she reasoned. And it would be pretty impressive if she was responsible for changing him. The thought of someone depending on her and needing her made her feel warm and safe—two things she hadn't felt in a very long time.

"Let's leave," Brian murmured. "People keep interrupting us and trying to lure you away from me. I don't want to take any more chances on losing you."

"Are you trying to kidnap me?" Enid asked teasingly.

"Yes," he answered, gazing intently into her eyes.

Her heart racing with excitement, Enid stepped out of his arms and gestured toward the door. "Let's take off, then."

Hand in hand, they made their way through the crowd. Enid avoided eye contact with anyone she knew.

"Catch you later, George," Brian called on the way out.

George Warren looked surprised. "Are you leaving with Brian, Enid?" he asked in a neutral voice.

Enid hitched her shoulder bag higher and lifted her chin. "Yes." She met his gaze defiantly.

George's eyes asked her if she knew what she was doing. Enid nodded. She could take care of herself.

"Merry Christmas, you guys," George said.

Brian draped one arm across her shoulders. "You didn't drive here, did you?"

Enid felt a momentary pang. She had come to the party with Jeffrey, and she hadn't even told him that she was leaving. Well, he wouldn't miss her, she was sure of that. He had Elizabeth to console him.

"No," she said.

"Good," Brian said. "If you had your own car, I'd have trouble kidnapping you."

In spite of herself, Enid laughed.

They got into his car, and Brian looked over at her before he started the ignition. "I really am sorry about last night," he said.

"It's all right," Enid reassured him. "I understand."

He gave her a wide smile and turned the key. "I was hoping you'd say that. See, the good thing about partying once in a while is that it keeps you from going totally overboard."

"The best way to keep from going overboard is not to party at all," Enid replied. "Just keep away from alcohol and drugs. Period."

"Oh, come on, Enid," Brian teased. "You're mature enough to know that you don't have to live like a monk. You just have to know how to handle it."

Enid looked at him skeptically. "And you can handle it?"

"Maybe I didn't last night," Brian said, grinning. "But I can. I know you can, too. The thing about you is, you've been through so much. You're much smarter than most girls your age, much more together. That's what I like about you. I really admire you, Enid."

"Oh, come on," Enid said.

"I do, honest." Brian put his hand on her shoulder and gave it a gentle squeeze. "You're a really special person."

Enid gazed ahead, letting Brian's compliments wash over her like a caressing wave. Half of her knew that everything he was saying was just flattery, but half of her liked it. After all, nobody else had made the effort to flatter her lately, except, of course, to tell her what a good friend she was. Deep inside, Enid wanted very much to believe Brian. She wanted to believe he really thought that she was special. She began to wonder what it would be like to get into a relationship with Brian. It would be difficult once he went back to Colorado at the end of winter break. But if there was really something between them, a relationship could work.

"Where are we going?" she asked, snapping back to the present.

Brian switched on the radio and threw her a lazy smile. "I thought we could go up to Miller's Point. I haven't been there in so long, and I was feeling kind of homesick for the old place."

Enid's pulse raced when Brian mentioned Miller's Point, a notorious make-out spot on a bluff overlooking the valley. She wasn't completely sure that she wanted to go up there with him, but she wasn't completely sure that she didn't.

They didn't speak for the rest of the way. Enid sank into the corner, deep in thought. From time to time she glanced at Brian's profile. There was no question about how good-looking he was. But even if they did have a future, she thought that he was rushing things a little bit.

Well, we don't have to stay at Miller's Point for very long, she thought.

"Here we are," Brian said as he parked the car.

They were silent for a moment, listening to "Silent Night" on the car's radio. Enid gazed up at the stars.

"It's Christmas Eve," she whispered. With everything that had been going on, the meaning of the holiday had almost been eclipsed.

"Merry Christmas," Brian said in a husky voice. He pulled her close and kissed her.

Enid tipped her head back and closed her eyes. Though Brian was a good kisser, Enid didn't feel anything.

It's just a first kiss, she thought. *It doesn't have to be like an earthquake.*

But she was a bit disappointed. She tried to convince herself that she was enjoying herself, but she really wasn't.

"What's wrong?" Brian asked, pulling away. He stroked her cheek.

Enid lowered her gaze. "Nothing."

"You seem a little nervous. That's OK. You just need to relax."

"I'm relaxed, really," Enid said quickly.

Brian reached over to open the glove compartment. He took out a small plastic bag.

"This will help," he said, pulling out a joint.

Alarm bells went off in Enid's head. "Brian, I told you before, I don't—"

"Come on." Brian laughed. "I thought we agreed that all you need to do is know how to handle it. You're no lightweight. You can deal with it."

"But I don't *want* to deal with it," Enid protested.

Brian flicked a lighter and dragged heavily on the joint until it flared up. A wisp of smoke curled up from the end and spiraled slowly over to Enid.

"One little joint," Brian coaxed. "It's not like you'll go haywire. It's just a relaxant. Like the way some people have a drink before dinner. That's all."

Enid breathed in the sweet scent of the pot smoke. Brian's words were dangerously convincing. And besides, the way her vacation was going, she deserved a chance to relax and to forget about things for a while.

"Here," Brian said, holding it out to her.

"I don't know." Enid shook her head slowly.

"Listen, you need this, I can tell," Brian said gently. "It'll be fine."

Sighing, Enid looked up and met Brian's eyes. He smiled and nodded.

"Oh, all right," she said. "What have I got to lose?"

Twelve

Enid inhaled deeply, then held the smoke in her lungs. The smell and taste of the marijuana transported her back to her past, and she started to feel sad. Even though she had changed her life, it was not really any better. Maybe it would never be any better.

"Here," she said, handing the joint back to Brian. Enid exhaled and gazed forlornly out at the stars.

"What's wrong?" Brian asked. He squinted against the smoke as he dragged on the joint again. "You look so down all of a sudden."

Enid shook her head and sank down in the seat. "I've had the worst week you could imagine," she complained. She took the joint back from Brian and inhaled. Self-pity threatened to overwhelm her.

Brian stroked her hair.

"It's my mother, for one thing," Enid explained sadly. "My folks are divorced," she went on. "And my mother is always on my dad's case. All we do lately is argue. She doesn't understand me."

"I know what you mean." Brian nodded wisely. "My mother's totally uncool, too."

Enid frowned. Brian couldn't understand completely. Nobody could.

"She doesn't want me to spend time with my father," Enid continued. "And she gets angry whenever he calls. Then he gets totally depressed."

"Right," Brian agreed. "Who wouldn't?"

"He got so upset today that he got plastered before noon. We were supposed to have lunch." Enid sniffled and thought of her father slurring his speech. She wished she could blot the memory out of her mind forever.

Brian carefully tapped ash off the end of the joint. "My old man is the same way. He gets so drunk some nights, he can't even use the remote control for the TV." Brian started to laugh.

"Yeah, well, it's not that funny," Enid said

indignantly. Suddenly, her head felt three sizes too big. "That's pretty strong dope."

Brian grinned. "It's good, isn't it? I know this guy at school who gets the finest Colombian weed. But you're cool, don't worry."

Enid leaned her head back and looked out of the passenger window. She wondered what Elizabeth would say if she could see her now.

"Hey," Brian interrupted her thoughts. "Why so serious?"

"My best friend." Enid explained. "She's so perfect, sometimes I want to scream. And she's not *really* all that perfect," she went on.

Brian nodded.

"Life is really unfair, isn't it?" Enid sighed heavily and tried to wet her lips. Her mouth was as dry as dust. "I wish I had something to drink," she said irritably.

"Did I hear you say drink? Just hang on a second." Brian leaned over the back of the seat and reached for something. When he sat back down, he had a fifth of bourbon in his hand. "We aim to please."

Enid eyed the bottle dubiously. The car was filled with smoke, and she was already much more high than she had expected to be. Drinking would only make things worse.

"Go ahead," Brian urged, pressing the bottle

into her hand. "Everything looks better when you have a little buzz on."

"Yeah." Enid made a sour face and uncapped the bottle. She took a swallow. The bourbon burned in her throat and seared a path all the way to her stomach. "Phew," she gasped. Her face felt hot and flushed.

Brian took the bottle from her and took three long swallows. The radio was playing "O Little Town of Bethlehem," and Brian said scornfully, "What *is* this trash, anyway? It's so corny."

"I like it," Enid said, suddenly feeling sentimental. "Don't change the station."

Enid felt lightheaded but she didn't feel any happier. The future looked so bleak and empty that she started to cry. "Nobody cares about me!"

Brian looked exasperated. "Oh, come on. Lighten up, Enid. You're acting like a kid."

"Sorry," Enid said, wiping her nose. "It's just—I don't know. Everything's so terrible."

"Here." Brian handed the bottle back to her, and she took a long swallow. "That's better," he said encouragingly.

Enid tried to focus on Brian's face. Everything was swimming in front of her eyes. "Why am I doing this? What am I doing here?" Enid asked suddenly.

"You're here because you need to party, that's why," Brian told her. "It's Christmas Eve, holiday time. Everyone parties on the holidays."

"Like the twelve days of Christmas? Is that what they're for?" she asked.

For some reason Enid felt the urgent need to know the answer to that question. Nothing was so important to her as knowing what the twelve days of Christmas were for. She was sure that if she could find the answer, everything else would make sense.

"Right," Brian said. He held the bottle aloft in a toast. "On the first day of Christmas, my toor love said to me—"

"Toor love?" Enid cut in, smiling. "That's not right."

"It's true love," Brian said in a serious voice, enunciating carefully. "True love. That's very important in this life."

Enid struggled to sit up straight and began to sing. "On the first day of Christmas my true love gave to me, a partridge in a bear tree."

"No!" Brian started laughing. "Wait a second. It's not—"

"Bear tree." Enid giggled. "Don't you know what a bear tree is? It's a tree with bears in it."

"OK, OK," Brian said. "On the second day

of Christmas my true love gave to me, two—two—what is it?"

Enid shrugged. "I don't know. Oh! Turtles, I mean turldoves. *Turtle*doves." It was hard to get her tongue to cooperate.

"That's wrong," Brian said, a big smile on his face. "It's turtle*dives*. That's like a cannonball."

Enid let out a scream of laughter. Life really *was* better this way. Everything was much more fun, much more cheerful. "You're so funny," she gasped.

Then, slowly, her smile faded.

Jessica gave Steven a pointed look. "I think Cara's looking for you."

"Huh?" Steven looked puzzled for a moment, and then he smiled. "Oh, right. I'll see you guys later."

When her brother had gone, Jessica turned her attention back to Steven's friend Michael. "Tell me more about your art history class."

"You don't really want to hear about that," Michael said, his eyes twinkling.

Jessica grinned. After only fifteen minutes, she knew that she had found a terrific guy. "I don't?"

"No, you don't," Michael replied. He stood

up and held out his hand. "You probably want to dance, right?"

"How did you ever guess?" Jessica twined her fingers with his. "You must be a mind reader."

"I'm taking a course in that, too," he said.

Jessica felt her heart give a little flutter. She was thrilled that she had actually found someone cute, interesting, and *interested*. When she had asked Steven to introduce them, Michael's blue eyes had lit up like stars. It was nice to know there were *some* boys at the party who weren't chasing Enid Rollins. Jessica felt a warm glow that had nothing to do with the spirit of Christmas.

"So why didn't Steven ever tell me he had such a cute sister?" Michael asked at they started to dance.

"He's very absentminded that way," Jessica said, shaking her head sadly. "Poor me. I never get to meet anyone or go anywhere."

Michael laughed. "Yeah, sure. You probably already have a boyfriend."

"Do you see a boyfriend around here?" Jessica gave him an innocent smile. "It's just lonely old me."

"Too bad," he murmured. "I take pity on you, Jessica."

"Thanks," she said. "I appreciate it."

Smiling, Michael pulled her close for a slow dance, and Jessica snuggled against him. The evening was definitely improving, she thought.

"It's warm in here, isn't it?" she asked softly.

"Sure is." Another couple bumped into them, and Michael said, "Crowded, too."

Jessica felt a rush of triumph. "Maybe we should take a break from the crowd," she suggested.

"Good idea." Michael took her hand, and they wove their way among the dancing couples, down the hall, and out through the back door. They wandered slowly across the darkened patio.

Jessica took a deep breath. "It's so nice out here."

"Mmm. It is."

"Aren't the stars beautiful?" Jessica strolled away, then turned and looked intently at Michael. "I know a place that has a much better view."

Michael leaned against the picnic table and folded his arms. His face was in shadow, but Jessica could tell that he was smiling at her. "Where is it?" he asked.

"Not far. We can just take a little drive, look at the stars, and come back."

"Sounds good." Michael held out his hand for hers. "Let's get out of here."

"I'll give you directions," Jessica said as they got into his car.

"Don't tell me," he said. "I bet I know where we're going. After all, I grew up near Sweet Valley," Michael grinned, and Jessica had a strong urge to reach over and brush his wavy brown hair out of his eyes. But she held back. Once they got to Miller's Point, there would be time enough. . . .

"I guess you *do* know the way," she said as they turned up the narrow road to the point. "And wasn't I right? Isn't the view great from up here?"

"Fantastic," he agreed.

When they reached the bluff overlooking the valley, Michael pulled the car in next to another one. "Someone else likes a scenic view as much as we do," he observed.

Jessica scooted a little closer to him. "So, what should we talk about?" she asked in a sultry voice.

Michael put his arm around her. "Well, let me see . . ."

Just then, they were shocked by a blast of music from the next car. The occupants had obviously turned the volume up suddenly, and the bass pounded like a hammer.

"Kind of loud, isn't it?" Michael asked.

Jessica tried to ignore it. She didn't want anything to spoil the romantic mood. "I don't hear anything," she whispered.

"Yeah, but—" Michael rolled his window down and peered at the other car. "They must be drunk."

Restraining an impatient sigh, Jessica slid across the seat and opened her door. "I'll be right back," she said.

Jessica marched over to the other car and rapped on the passenger window. If they wanted to play music, there were better places to do it than at Miller's Point, she thought. Especially when she was trying to concentrate on something *important*.

"Hey!" she shouted. It was too dark for Jessica to tell how many people were in the car. She banged on the window again. "Turn it down!"

When there was still no response, Jessica yanked on the door. Music thundered out, and in the glare of the overhead light, Jessica saw Enid Rollins and Brian Saunders. An empty liquor bottle was on the seat between them, and a thick haze of smoke drifted out into the night air. Jessica was so stunned that she couldn't speak.

"What? Jessica?" Enid mumbled. "Oh, no." She turned her head away.

"Enid!" Jessica gasped. She stared at the couple for several moments. "Are you drunk?"

"No," Enid whispered

Without another word, Jessica turned and hurried back to Michael's car.

"Let's go," she said, climbing in.

He was startled. "Where?"

Jessica's mind was spinning. "Back to the party."

Thirteen

Mrs. Rollins finished the crossword puzzle she was working on and checked her watch for what seemed like the twentieth time. It worried her that Enid wasn't back from the party yet. It wasn't really late, only ten-thirty, but Enid had promised to be home by ten to spend part of Christmas Eve with her mother.

Mrs. Rollins stood up and crossed the living room to the Christmas tree. The tiny lights blinked cheerfully, heating the branches so that they gave off a rich, spicy scent. She fingered one of the ornaments, a shiny angel blowing a trumpet. It had always been Enid's favorite, the first to go on the tree in a yearly family ritual.

But this year it had seemed as though Enid had helped with the decorating more out of habit than out of pleasure. Mrs. Rollins knew that Enid was hurting lately, and she knew that she had a lot to do with her daughter's pain.

"Oh, Enid, what am I doing wrong?" she murmured. "I'm doing my best, I really am. It's just so hard."

The ringing of the telephone broke the silence, and Mrs. Rollins hurried to answer it.

"Mrs. Rollins? This is Liz."

"Hi, Liz," she said, suddenly worried. "What is it?"

"I was hoping I could talk to Enid about something. I know it's late, but it's really important."

The words sent a ripple of anxiety through Mrs. Rollins. She tried to keep her voice calm. "She's not here, Liz. Wasn't she at the party with you?"

"Well, I'm actually still at George's house. Enid left here about an hour ago." Elizabeth paused. "I thought she'd be home by now."

Mrs. Rollins shook her head. "No. Was Jeffrey bringing her home? He picked her up earlier this evening."

"No. She left with a boy I don't know. His name is Brian."

"Brian? Brian Saunders?" Mrs. Rollins sat down heavily. "He's—he's someone Enid used to know. He's not a boy she should be with now." All of the helplessness she had felt during Enid's trouble with drugs came flooding back.

"I'm sure she'll be home any minute," Elizabeth said hopefully. "Would you ask her to call me at home when she gets in?"

"I will. Thanks, Liz."

She hung up and began to pace the room. For a moment, she considered calling the police. But it wouldn't do any good to imagine the worst. Enid and Brian had probably just stopped somewhere for a bite to eat, or a walk on the beach. Still, just this morning Enid had told her that she had had a terrible time with Brian. Why would Enid have left the party with him?

Mrs. Rollins heard a car pull up outside the house. With a gasp of relief, she ran to the front door and opened it.

Her ex-husband was walking up to the door.

"Hello, Adele," he said quietly. "I hope it's not too late to drop in. I have to talk to Enid, and it can't wait until tomorrow."

Mrs. Rollins shook her head. Her lips were dry, and she licked them nervously. "She's not home," she said, hoping her voice sounded steady.

"On Christmas Eve?" Mr. Rollins looked surprised. "But where—"

"I'm not sure where she is." Her voice cracked as she answered, and she beckoned with her hand. "Come on in, David."

"Did she go out?"

"She went to a party with her friends from school. I just got a call from Elizabeth. She told me that Enid left an hour ago with someone she knew when she was into drugs," Mrs. Rollins explained. "Enid told me that he's still wild and I'm worried. She was so upset today, I just don't know . . ."

Mr. Rollins sat down on the couch and put his head on his hands. "It's my fault that she's upset," he said painfully. "If she's gone off and done something foolish, I'll never forgive myself."

"Don't blame yourself, Dave," Mrs. Rollins urged. "And don't jump to conclusions, either. We just have to figure out what to do—if there *is* something we can do."

"Where would they go? Who is this kid she's with? Do you know his parents?" Mr. Rollins demanded.

"I don't know him very well. Please don't yell at me, Dave. I'm trying to think." She put one hand nervously to her forehead. "There were a few places where Enid used to go with that old crowd. I didn't think she would ever go back to them, but—"

"Where? Just tell me and I'll look for her."

Mrs. Rollins hesitated. She felt terrible, suspecting Enid of so easily falling back into her old ways. She knew that she should trust her daughter to be strong. But she also knew that Enid had been very upset recently, and that she could be vulnerable to someone's bad influence.

"The party is at George Warren's house on Hacienda Street, but she's not there anymore. You could try Kelly's," she said in a quavery voice. "That's out on the state road. And there was a place on Fourth Street called the Pink Lady, or something like that."

"I'll go." Mr. Rollins headed for the door. "I'll call you in half an hour to see if she's home." He paused and looked back. Adele Rollins looked shaken, and he felt a wave of regret. "I'll bring her back, Adele. I swear it."

Mr. Rollins ran back to his car and got behind the wheel. His head was pounding, both from a hangover and from anxiety. Waves of guilt rippled through him.

"I'm sorry, honey. I'm so sorry," he whispered.

He started the car and headed for Kelly's. He

wished he could turn the clock back to that morning and start all over. He knew he couldn't go back, but at least he could help Enid now. If only he knew where she was.

Several beat-up cars were parked randomly outside Kelly's, a sleazy hangout on the edge of town. Mr. Rollins went inside. He looked around for Enid, but she wasn't there. The sight of the solitary drinkers leaning on the bar made him feel sick all of a sudden. He knew that he was seeing a vision of what he could become, and it scared him.

He was shaking when he got back into his car. There was a small flask of gin in the glove compartment. Mr. Rollins angrily threw it out the window. It smashed into glittering fragments on the pavement.

"No more," he said through clenched teeth.

He owed it to his daughter to shape up, and more than anything else, he wanted to tell her that.

But first he had to find her.

Enid tried to shake the fog from her head. Things seemed to be happening in slow motion. "Jessica?" she said fuzzily. "That was Jessica Wakefield. Where did she go?"

Brian was slumped in his seat, rhythmically tapping his fingers on the steering wheel and humming loudly to the sound of the radio.

"Where did she go?" Enid repeated. She stepped out of the car unsteadily and squinted hard to make the world stop weaving back and forth. She wasn't even sure that Jessica had really been there—she could have imagined her.

But Enid knew that she hadn't.

"No! No! No!" Enid cried, leaning back against the car door.

The cool night air was sobering her up by small degrees, and a crashing wave of humiliation engulfed her. To be seen in this condition was unbelievably bad—and to be seen by Jessica Wakefield! It wouldn't be long before everyone knew that Enid had been stoned out of her mind with Brian Saunders. She wanted the earth to open up and swallow her. Enid crawled back into the car.

"Take me home," she said thickly. "I have to go home. Brian!" Enid jostled his shoulder.

"What?" he snapped. He raised his head and looked at her blearily. "What are you talking about?"

"I want to go home," Enid said. She knew that she was about to be sick to her stomach.

Brian laughed. "You're kidding me. You can't just go home now."

"Why not?" Enid whispered. The nausea was almost overpowering. She swallowed hard a few times and tried to look at him. He appeared very far away, and Enid rubbed her eyes.

"You wanted to come up here as much as I did," he replied. "Are you some kind of a tease, leading me on like that?"

Enid stared at him. "No—I never meant—I just want to go home," she said. "Please take me home."

"Forget it." Brian picked up the empty bourbon bottle and tipped it up to his mouth. When nothing came out, he tossed it out the window and swore under his breath.

Enid was sobering up fast. "Take me home, Brian. I mean it. I want to leave."

"You really want to leave?"

Enid nodded. The look in Brian's eyes made her very nervous. Even through a fog of drugs and alcohol, Enid felt like the biggest idiot in the world for having placed even a shred of confidence in his phony clean-and-sober act.

"We'll leave." Brian fumbled with the car keys and finally succeeded in starting the engine. Without looking, he backed up at top speed, jerked the steering wheel around, and slammed the car into drive.

Enid gripped the armrest. She realized that Brian was in no condition to drive. He was even more drunk than she was.

"I'm getting out," she said.

"No way." Brian stepped on the gas, and Enid was thrown back against the seat.

The car swerved wildly from lane to lane as they raced down the highway. Enid felt as if she were in a nightmare. "Slow down," she begged.

"I told you, I can handle it." Brian laughed. He turned the radio up to full volume again.

Brian could barely control the car. His head swayed back and forth, and with each bump in the road, he sent the steering wheel into a swooping turn.

"Let's stop at Kelly's and shake the place up!" he shouted.

"Just stop the car," Enid pleaded, closing her eyes as the guardrail loomed up alongside them.

"Relax," Brian said. "You're no fun to party with anymore, Enid. You're a real drag."

"Then take me home!" Enid shouted.

The headlights flashed briefly on a stop sign before Brian drove past it. Another car missed them by only a yard.

Enid moaned. She was sure that they were going to crash and die.

"Let's go back to that party and get things going!" Brian said.

"*No!*" Enid screamed. "Just take me home!"

"Well, we're going to have a little fun whether you want to or not," Brian said, stepping on the gas again. "Time for a little Christmas cheer!"

Enid had a terrible feeling that this was the last Christmas she would ever see.

Fourteen

"Who *was* that back there?" Michael asked as they pulled up in front of George's house.

"I told you, just somebody I know," Jessica replied hastily.

She could hardly wait to get inside and drop her bombshell. Enid Rollins, an empty liquor bottle, a stoned date! No wonder Enid hadn't wanted to talk about Brian Saunders the other day at the mall!

"It looks as though a lot of people have already left," Michael observed.

"Not too many, I hope." Jessica ran ahead of him to the house and burst inside.

"Where's Lila?" she asked Ken Matthews, who was standing right inside the door.

Ken shrugged. "I don't know. Around, I guess."

Jessica hurried into the living room. She felt a little badly that things hadn't worked out with Michael this evening, but there would be time for romance later. After all, gossip was gossip!

"Jessica?"

At the sound of her sister's voice she spun around, trying to keep the eager smile off her face. "Hey, Liz, I was just looking for you."

"You were?" Elizabeth looked worried and distracted. "I don't know what to do," she said under her breath.

"About what?" Jessica asked impatiently.

"It's Enid. I don't know where she is. She left here over an hour ago with some guy named Brian Saunders. He's bad news, Jess. I called Enid's house, and she's still not home. Now I'm wondering if something's happened to her."

Jessica couldn't believe her luck. Elizabeth had just given her the perfect opening. But she could not appear to be thrilled by her news about Enid. She would have to appear shocked. Actually it *was* shocking, Jessica thought. And she was the one who had the answer about where Enid was!

"Well, as a matter of fact—" she began.

A commotion at the door interrupted her. Annoyed, Jessica looked to see what all the noise was about.

"Has Enid Rollins come back here tonight?" a tall, frantic-looking man asked the group.

"Mr. Rollins!" Elizabeth hurried over to him.

"Hello, Elizabeth. Enid left with some boy, didn't she? Has she come back?"

Jessica watched in satisfaction as a crowd formed around Mr. Rollins, talking animatedly and offering suggestions. Jessica waited until there was a moment's lull, and then she stepped forward to make her announcement.

"I just saw her a few minutes ago," she said into the silence.

Instantly everyone turned to stare at her. It was as though she had just flipped a switch; the effect was almost electrical. Jeffrey pushed his way toward Jessica in order to hear her better. Jessica felt another twinge of satisfaction. Jeffrey wouldn't be so interested in Enid when he found out what kind of girl she *really* was under all that sweetness and light.

"Where was she?" Mr. Rollins demanded.

"Up at Miller's Point." Jessica made sure that she had a properly concerned expression on her face as she added, "And I really hate to say this, but I think she might have been a little bit—under the influence."

Elizabeth stared at her sister in amazement. "What exactly do you mean, 'under the influence'?"

"You know, drunk." Jessica shook her head sorrowfully.

"Are they still up there?" Mr. Rollins asked in an anguished voice.

Jessica shrugged. "I don't know. They were still there when I left."

"You just *left* her there?" Elizabeth demanded. "You just drove away? Why didn't you take her home, Jessica?"

"Oh, God," Mr. Rollins said as he turned and rushed out to the street.

Suddenly it dawned on Jessica that her friends were staring at her in anger, and she felt a jolt of panic and shame. Just because she had been jealous of Brian's and Jeffrey's interest in Enid, she had chosen to hurt her sister's best friend instead of helping her. Now she realized that by leaving Enid with Brian she had done a truly terrible thing.

"Oh, no," she whispered, shaking her head. "I wasn't thinking."

"You *never* think, Jessica!" Elizabeth snapped

at her. She grabbed her jacket and looked at Jeffrey. "Come on. We have to find her."

"I'm coming, too!" Jessica cried. She bumped into Lila as she followed the others to the door. "Come with me," she pleaded.

When Jessica and Lila joined Elizabeth and Jeffrey on the sidewalk, Elizabeth turned on her angrily. "Now what? Do you want to embarrass her even more?"

"I'm sorry!" Jessica replied. "I want to help."

"Let's just get out of here," Jeffrey said, yanking open the door of his car.

The other three piled in, and Jeffrey made a squealing U-turn to follow Mr. Rollins's car.

"How are we going to find them?" Elizabeth asked fearfully. "They might not even be up at Miller's Point anymore."

"We'll find them," Jeffrey replied firmly.

In the backseat, Jessica sank into the corner. She knew that if anything happened to Enid, everyone would blame her.

I didn't make her drunk, though, she reminded herself. *And if I hadn't seen Enid and come back to tell everyone, no one would know where to start looking for her.*

As much as that was true, Jessica still felt very guilty. She should have taken Enid home or have stayed with her—anything except what she did do—leave her behind. Enid wasn't all that bad. And Elizabeth would be devastated if anything happened to her best friend. Tears began to roll down Jessica's face as the car raced through the darkness of Christmas Eve.

We have to find them, she thought. *We just have to find them.*

Brian was racing the car around an empty parking lot, periodically hitting the brakes to make the car spin around.

"This is outrageous!" Brian yelled.

Enid's heart was pounding so loudly in her ears, she thought that she would go deaf. She was beyond pleading with Brian. She just prayed that he would use up his energy racing around the empty parking lot and that he wouldn't get back on the highway. And she held on to the hope that he would slow down just long enough for her to jump out of the car.

But Brian was far from ready to quit. He swung the car out of the parking lot.

"What—where are we going?" Enid cried.

"Back where we started," Brian said. "Back up to Miller's Point!"

"No, please take me home! Or just stop and let me out!"

Brian laughed. "No way. I just remembered something. I have another bottle of bourbon in the trunk!"

The car barreled down the street. Brian sang loudly to the radio, and he took a corner at fifty miles an hour, sideswiping two cars parked along the curb. Enid screamed and closed her eyes. The crunch and scrape of metal vibrated in her bones. Brian cheered riotously and pressed his foot on the gas pedal.

Enid cowered in her seat. The knot of fear in her stomach was growing tighter and tighter.

Why did I do this? she wondered. *How could I let myself do this? Nothing is so bad that I have to end up this way. I want to go home! I want to go home!*

"Stop the car, Brian!" she commanded in the sternest voice she could muster. "Stop the car right now! I mean it! We're already in so much trouble. Don't you know what you did to those cars?"

Brian grinned at her and put one hand over his eyes. "Be nice, or I won't watch the road," he taunted.

Enid was afraid to say anything more. In his state, if Brian got angry, there was no telling what he might do. Instead, she just stared silently ahead, a plan forming in her mind. If they could just get safely back to Miller's Point, she could run away, as soon as Brian stopped the car.

"Why are you being such a drag, Enid? You used to be a lot of fun." Brian veered off the highway onto the narrow road that led to Miller's Point. "*I'm* having a blast. What's a little fender bender? It's not the end of the world. Who's even going to know who did it? I can't believe you turned out to be such a wimp."

"That's right, Brian, I am a wimp," Enid said tightly. "I don't see why you want me to stay with you. Just let me out here."

"Sorry," he said. "Can't do that. Can't have a party with just one person, you know."

The road ahead curved dangerously uphill. Brian was going eighty miles per hour. Enid squeezed her eyes shut. When she opened them again, her heart leapt in terror. Another car was coming toward them in the opposite lane, but Brian was driving in the middle of the road.

"Move over!" Enid yelled.

"He'll move first." Brian narrowed his eyes and pressed down on the accelerator. "He'll chicken out before I do."

Enid reached for the steering wheel and tried to yank it toward her. Brian pushed her away, and they struggled. The oncoming car blared its horn and swerved aside just as Brian cut the steering wheel sharply to the right.

The car smashed into the guardrail with a deafening crunch, tore through it, and flipped over. Enid closed her eyes at the first bone-jarring thud.

Fifteen

Enid tried to wake up, but her arms and legs felt as heavy as lead. She heard groaning and thought that it might be her own, but she couldn't be sure. She knew somehow that it was important for her to wake up. Finally she opened her eyes. The car was upside down, and she was held in place by her seat belt. The smell of gasoline made her gag.

"Enid? ENID!"

There was a furious tapping on the glass by her head. She wished that it would stop, but it wouldn't. Slowly she turned her head to see what was making the noise. It was her father, and he was upside-down. Confused, she closed her eyes.

"Unlock the door!" he yelled beyond the glass. "Enid, Hurry!"

Enid opened her eyes but couldn't move.

"Enid! Unlock the door right now!"

Enid managed to get her fingers under the lock button. It popped up suddenly, and her father yanked the door open. He unfastened the seat belt, and Enid's head hit the top of the car. She half fell and was half dragged from the car.

"Enid! Oh, thank God!" Mr. Rollins cried, gathering her into his arms.

"Daddy," she whispered. Tears began to run down her face, and racking sobs shook her body. Pain was beginning to slice through the fog in her head. "Daddy! It hurts!"

"I know, sweetie," he answered tearfully as he carried her away from the wreck.

Tires squealed on the road above as another car braked to a stop. Doors slammed and voices shouted in the dark. Enid knew that her father was carrying her away, up a steep bank.

"Enid!" Elizabeth cried. "Is she all right?"

Enid tried to raise her head. "Liz?" she asked groggily. Arms came out to help her, and she was gently lowered to the grass.

"Enid!" Elizabeth cried. "Oh, thank God you're alive."

"I'm OK," she whispered. "Where's my father?"

"He went back for Brian," Jessica answered in a frightened voice.

"I'll go help." Jeffrey began to scramble down the steep bank.

"Stay back!" Mr. Rollins yelled. "It's going to blow!"

"DADDY!" Enid screamed, struggling wildly against Elizabeth's arms. "DADDY!"

Mr. Rollins fought to open the driver's door, but it was stuck. He ran around to the passenger side and crawled in after Brian.

"He's got him!" Lila gasped. "He's dragging him away from the—"

A deafening explosion cut off her sentence. Enid, lying on the grass, closed her eyes and began to shake uncontrollably.

A roaring inferno bloomed behind Enid's eyes. Someone covered her with a jacket, and then she blacked out. When she opened her eyes again, Elizabeth was leaning over her. A paramedic with a stethoscope was listening to her heart. Enid heard a wailing noise, and realized that it was a siren and that they were in an ambulance.

"It's OK, Enid." Tears streaked Elizabeth's face, and she gripped Enid's hand tightly. "You're going to be OK."

"Excuse me," the paramedic said quietly to Elizabeth, as he put a blood-pressure cuff around Enid's arm. She stared at the ceiling of the ambulance. There was something she wanted to say, but her head hurt so much that she couldn't remember what it was. She tried to clear her throat.

"Liz? What—?" Her eyes closed, but she forced them open again. "Liz?"

And then she lost consciousness again.

Everything was very quiet, Enid felt she was floating on a soft current. Slowly she became aware that someone was holding her wrist.

"Where am I?" Enid asked, opening her eyes.

A nurse in a white uniform was standing beside her. A dim light from a bedside lamp fell across her face. Even the faint glow hurt Enid's eyes.

"You're at the hospital," the nurse said softly. "You've hurt your head, but you'll be fine after you get some rest. Don't try to talk."

Enid wanted to be polite and cooperative, so

she closed her eyes. But she knew that there was still something she wanted to ask.

"My father!" she gasped, trying to sit up.

"Shh!" The nurse pushed her gently down on the bed. "He's in the burn-care unit. He received some bad burns, but the doctors are taking care of him. They're taking care of your boyfriend, too."

"He's not my boyfriend," Enid muttered. "My father—is he hurt bad?"

The nurse put a cool hand on Enid's forehead. "He'll be fine. Don't worry. Just try to sleep."

"It's my fault," Enid cried weakly. "It's all my fault."

"Shh," the nurse whispered. "Just lie quietly for now."

Enid fell back to sleep with tears on her lashes.

Mrs. Rollins ran to the hospital reception desk. "Where's my daughter?" she panted. "Enid Rollins?"

The night nurse, who was wearing a small Santa Claus pin on her uniform, consulted a computer screen. Christmas carols played softly over the P.A. system. "Room three-fifteen," she said. "Stop at the nurse's station on the third floor for an update on her condition."

Nodding her thanks, Mrs. Rollins hurried to the elevator. When the doors slid open on the third floor, Elizabeth was the first person she saw.

"Liz!" she exclaimed. "How is she?"

Elizabeth ran over to Mrs. Rollins and gave her a comforting hug. "The doctor says Enid will be OK—nothing's broken, and she doesn't have any internal injuries. I think she's sleeping right now."

Mrs. Rollins's heart was pounding wildly as she walked down the hall. As quietly as she could, she pushed open the door to her daughter's room. Enid was asleep, a bandage wrapped around her head. Soft light fell on her face from a shaded lamp. She looked very small and very young.

"Oh, baby," Mrs. Rollins whispered, sitting on the bed at Enid's side. She took her daughter's hand and kissed it gently.

There was a light tap on the door. A tired-looking man with a stethoscope around his neck opened the door. "Mrs. Rollins?"

She stood up quickly. "Yes?"

"Dr. Meyerson," he said, shaking her hand.

"Let me reassure you, your daughter will be fine. Her X-rays are normal."

"But what happened?" Mrs. Rollins asked. "All I was told was that there was an accident."

Dr. Meyerson nodded. "The car Brian Saunders and your daughter were driving in smashed through a guardrail and overturned."

Mrs. Rollins felt her stomach roll over. She closed her eyes for a moment. "And?"

"And your husband got them both out. But he and the Saunders boy both received some bad burns when the car exploded. They're in the burn-care unit."

Mrs. Rollins shuddered.

Dr. Meyerson stopped and looked closely at her. "Are you all right? It's not been a very nice Christmas Eve for you."

"I'm fine," she replied, managing to smile. "Enid's alive. That's all that matters."

Enid opened her eyes. Had she been dreaming, or had she heard her mother call her name? The room was empty, but she could not shake the feeling that someone had been holding her hand. She wanted to see her mother and to apologize. And she wanted to see her father.

He had saved her life. Her father had saved her life and Brian's. There was no way that she could ever love him enough to repay him for what he had done.

Enid's heart ached with tenderness, love—and remorse. She turned her head restlessly as memories of the night with Brian began to overwhelm her.

I was drunk and I was stoned. How could I have done it? she asked herself miserably.

No one had to tell her how lucky she and Brian were to be alive. Most people ended up dead after drinking and driving.

Never again. Never, never, never, she told herself. One slipup was enough to tell her that going back to her old ways could only mean disaster. She had been spared this time, but she might not be the next time. She was so grateful to have been given another chance.

She wondered if Brian felt the same way she did. Being in a near-fatal accident should be enough to scare anyone into changing his or her life.

But some people would never change.

"Will you, Dad?" she whispered into the darkened room. Enid had to admit to herself that her father was an alcoholic. Now she finally really understood that his alcoholism was the main reason for her parents' divorce. Looking back over the years, Enid wondered how many times her father had been drunk, how many times her mother had tried to cover it up, and how many times she had pretended not to see. And she also wondered just how much of her own terrible experimentation with alcohol and drugs had been a desperate reaction to her father's destructive behavior.

Tears sprang to her eyes. She knew she was still weak and vulnerable from the accident, but the thought that her father might not want to change made her heart feel as if it were breaking. Her head began to pound again, and the ache spread down through her limbs. She felt broken and crushed in both body and spirit.

Sixteen

Enid woke up slowly to the warm scent of spruce needles and the sight of her mother sleeping in a chair by her bed. The Christmas tree from home stood in the corner of the room, twinkling with lights. She didn't know how it had gotten there. It seemed like magic.

"Mom?"

Mrs. Rollins woke up with a start. "Enid." She smiled tenderly. "How do you feel?"

"OK, I guess." Enid raised herself up and looked around. Her hospital room was transformed by flowers, wrapped presents, and Christmas decorations. Morning poured light in through the window. She smiled. "Is it Christmas?"

"Yes, Enid. Merry Christmas, sweetheart."

Adele Rollins leaned over the bed to give her daughter a hug and a kiss.

"I'm sorry, Mom," Enid whispered, holding her mother tightly.

"Shh. It's OK. Whatever happens, we can handle it."

"You know, it's funny." Enid sniffled. "Being in the hospital on Christmas should make me feel sad, but I feel so happy."

"Me, too." Mrs. Rollins sat down on the bed and wiped her eyes.

Enid looked into her mother's eyes. "Mom, I did something terrible last night. I was feeling so sorry for myself that I got wasted. I can't believe that I was so weak. It will never, never happen again, I promise."

"I know it won't, Enid." Mrs. Rollins reached for a small box wrapped in shiny green paper. "I want you to open this right now. Go on."

"For me?" Smiling eagerly Enid tore the wrapping paper off the box and opened it. Nestled inside on the cotton was a gold heart on a chain. Her own heart swelled with love and gratitude.

"Oh, Mom," she breathed. The gold heart

caught the morning light in soft, warm glints. "It's beautiful."

"Here, I'll help you put it on." Mrs. Rollins undid the catch and fastened the pendant around Enid's neck. "It looks perfect on you," she said through tears of happiness.

"I'll never shut you out again, Mom," Enid promised, gripping her mother's hand tightly. "I don't want to lose you. From now on, I'll be honest about what I'm feeling."

Mrs. Rollins squeezed Enid's hand and shook her head. "What happened last night was my fault, too. I haven't been trying hard enough to understand what you've been going through, and I've been too stubborn to let go of my own anger, even for your sake."

"Oh, Mom—"

Before Enid could say anything more, there was a gentle knock on the door. "Come in."

Enid let out a gasp of surprise as Elizabeth, Jeffrey, Jessica, and Lila peeked in the room. "Hi!" she called out.

"Enid!" Elizabeth ran in and impulsively threw her arms around her. "Oh! Sorry, did I hurt you?"

Enid laughed. "No—I'm fine." She looked at the others happily. "I can't believe that you guys came here on Christmas morning!"

"Are you kidding?" Jeffrey retorted. "We've

been waiting for a half an hour for you to wake up!"

"And we brought Christmas to you," Jessica explained, pointing to the tree. "We lugged it over from your house last night."

Enid felt a faint flush warm her cheeks. She remembered that Jessica was the one who had seen her at her worst. When she looked at her, Jessica just smiled sheepishly and shrugged.

"Thanks," Enid said, overwhelmed with gratitude for her friends.

"And now you have to open your presents," Elizabeth said cheerfully. "Open mine first."

They were short a chair so Jeffrey went into the hall and came back in with a wheelchair. As he sat down in it, Enid noticed that his face had a drawn, tired look to it.

"You look like an invalid," Enid laughed.

"Yeah," Lila agreed, eyeing him critically. "You look worse than Enid does."

Elizabeth gasped and rolled her eyes. "You've got a great bedside manner, Lila."

"Let me see if I can find Enid something to eat," Mrs. Rollins said smiling. She left the room.

Elizabeth plumped up the pillows behind Enid's back, and the others piled their Christmas presents on her lap. Elizabeth's gift to her was a pretty fabric frame in which she had placed a photograph of the two of them at the beach. Enid felt a lump rise in her throat, and Elizabeth reached out to squeeze her hand.

"Here," Jessica said eagerly, handing Enid a small, oddly shaped package. "I picked it out for Liz, but she doesn't need any more presents from me. I want you to have it."

"But—" Enid sent her best friend an apologetic look. Elizabeth laughed. Enid unwrapped the package to find the pair of crazy sunglasses with pink palm trees along the upper rim. Enid put them on.

"How do I look?"

"Cool. Very cool," Jeffrey replied.

"They go great with that hospital gown," Lila added.

"Oh, Enid, before I forget, Todd called this morning." Elizabeth smiled. "He told me to give you a big kiss and a hug."

Enid glanced from Jeffrey to Elizabeth and back again. Jeffrey didn't seem the least bit uncomfortable at the mention of Todd's name. Was it possible that there really wasn't anything going on between Jeffrey and Elizabeth? She so wanted to ask, but she knew that now was not the time. Still, Enid glowed with happiness and hope, and she was glad that the sunglasses hid the sparkle in her eyes.

"Here we go," Mrs. Rollins called out, backing into the room with a tray in her hands. "Eggnog for everyone. And get ready, Enid. Your doctor said he'll be coming by in half an hour or so. I'm sure he'll want to poke at you."

"Let's hide her," Jessica suggested. "We'll all lie on top of the bed and say that we haven't seen her."

"Or we'll smuggle her out," Jeffrey said, laughing.

"Right," Elizabeth said. "You don't really need to stay here any longer. You're fine, aren't you?"

Enid grinned. She felt special and loved. "I *am* fine," she agreed. "I'm just fine."

"Let's have a toast," Lila said. "To a full recovery and a fantastic rest of the vacation."

As Enid looked at her mother and at her friends, she realized that it really was a wonderful Christmas, after all.

When Dr. Meyerson came to check on Enid, her friends waited outside in the hall. He pronounced her well enough to get out of bed and walk around when she felt like it, and her friends came barging back in.

After a laughter-filled hour, Enid's friends went home to their own families. Mrs. Rollins began to pick up crumpled wrapping paper and to throw out dirty plastic cups. As Enid watched her mother her, smile faded. The harsh reality of what had happened the night before came flooding back to her.

"Mom?" she asked quietly.

"Yes, honey?"

Enid bit her lip. "How's Dad? Do you know?"

"He is covered in gauze and bandages, and he may need some skin grafts, but he's going to be fine. If you feel up to it, I bet he'd love to see you," her mother said.

"He saved my life, didn't he?"

Mrs. Rollins nodded. "He would have walked through fire to save you—he very nearly did, too."

"Mom, I feel so terrible." Enid pressed her lips together to keep them from trembling. "He could have been killed!"

Her mother sat by her on the bed and took both her daughter's hands in her own. "Don't think about what might have happened. What matters is that you're both all right."

"I want to see Dad," Enid said, in spite of the fact that she was afraid—afraid that he would blame her, afraid that he was hurt worse than her mother and the nurse had told her.

"Go on," Mrs. Rollins said, patting her daughter's shoulder. "Go see him."

Enid slipped out of her bed and let her mother help her into her bathrobe. Her muscles still ached, but she felt strong enough to walk on her own.

"He's in the burn-care unit," Mrs. Rollins said, "which is right on this floor." Her mother reached down beside her bag, which was by her feet, and picked up a small package. "Here."

Enid saw that her mother was holding out the gift Enid had bought for her father. "You brought it!"

"Of course. He shouldn't have to miss Christmas just because he's in the hospital," her mother teased.

"I love you, Mom!" Enid gave her mother a heartfelt hug and headed for the burn unit. Her heart was beating hard. She took a deep breath, then pushed open the door and peeked in. "Dad?"

Mr. Rollins was sitting up in the bed. His bandaged arms were resting on top of the covers. Bandages partially covered his face. Enid felt a sob catch in her throat.

She rushed in and threw her arms around him. "Dad, I'm so sorry!" She burst into tears and pressed her face against his shoulder. "I'm so sorry!"

For several long moments they embraced in silence. Finally, Enid raised herself and looked into his eyes. She touched his forehead tenderly. "Dad, you look so silly," she said, half crying and half laughing.

"Is that any way to talk to your father?" he asked, and chuckled.

Enid shook her head. "Dad, if you hadn't come looking for me, I don't know what would have happened."

"But I did, and you're all right. The doctor told me that you just got banged up a bit."

"I'm fine, Dad," Enid said, sniffling.

"That's great." He took her hand and put it to his lips to kiss it. "And I want to tell you something. I've been lying here this morning thinking about myself and my life." Mr. Rollins looked at her squarely. "What I did to you yesterday when we were supposed to have lunch—"

"Forget it, Dad," Enid said hastily, blushing at the memory.

"No. Let me finish, Enid. When I realized last night how close I came to losing you, that was the last straw. I know I've got a real problem," he said, his voice shaky.

Enid tried to speak, but she couldn't.

"I have to admit it, and I have to do something about it. This morning I asked the doctor about a rehabilitation program, and he gave me the name of a good clinic. As soon as I'm out of the hospital, I'm checking into the clinic. And I promise you, I'm not coming out until I know I've licked this thing that has had such a hold on me. For your sake, Enid, and for my own, I am not going to end up living inside a bottle."

Enid felt tears come to her eyes, "It seems that all I do lately is cry," she said. "I'm so glad for you, Dad."

"It means that I won't be able to see you, or even to call you on the phone for a couple of months," he warned her. "It's a tough program. I'll do anything if it means I'll be clean when I come out."

"I'll be waiting, Dad," Enid promised. "And I'll never try to escape into drugs and alcohol again. Lately I was feeling as if everyone owed me something, and that only other people were making me unhappy and lonely. But *I'm* the only one who can make me happy. *I'm* the one who has to remember just how special I am."

Mr. Rollins smiled tenderly. "And I've got to finally accept the responsibility for my own happiness as well."

Enid hugged him again. "I hope you can take

something with you to the clinic." She held out the gift. "Here, Dad, I'll help you open it," Enid said, as Mr. Rollins fumbled with the paper.

Enid held her breath as he took out a key chain with a tiny picture frame dangling from the end. The picture was of Enid. "Do you like it?" she asked hopefully.

"Like it? I love it! Now I'll always have that stern expression of yours nearby to help keep me in line."

"Cut it out!" She giggled. "I don't look stern in that picture."

Mr. Rollins winked. "I know you don't. You look like my own little princess."

"Not that old princess bit again!"

"What can I say? I'm a foolish father, and I dote on my little girl. And I'm never, ever going to lose her again."

"We can make it together, Dad," Enid said. "Merry Christmas."

Seventeen

Jessica stood before the wall-to-wall mirror in Lila's bathroom and examined her eyelashes. Just a little more mascara and the effect would be perfect.

"Did we invite everyone?" Lila called from her big bedroom.

"Just about every single person we know," Jessica replied. She recapped the mascara and smiled at her reflection.

"Do you think Michael will come?" Lila asked.

Jessica grinned. "I would bet money on it. How could he *not* come to the best New Year's Eve party in Sweet Valley?" After what had happened on Christmas Eve, Jessica had thought that Michael would not want anything more to do with her. But he had called her during the week, and she had been honest with him about how sorry she was for having left Enid at Miller's Point. Michael had seemed to understand.

"Did you take my pink shoes?" Lila asked.

"Yes. You promised I could wear them." Jessica went to the bathroom door and gazed across the huge expanse of Lila's bedroom. Her friend was standing in front of her walk-in closet in her underwear. "Nice outfit, Lila."

Lila grinned and slipped a bright red dress off its hanger. "Think anyone would notice if I went downstairs like this?"

"No." Jessica shook her head solemnly and then burst out laughing. New Year's Eve was always so exciting, and having a party at Fowler Crest was the perfect way to ring out the old and ring in the new.

While Lila finished dressing, Jessica put on the neon-pink earrings Elizabeth had given her for Christmas. With her strapless pink dress and Lila's pink shoes, they looked fantastic. If Jessica's New Year's resolution came true, she would have Michael captivated by the end of the evening.

"Come on, let's finish putting up the decorations," Lila said.

The girls ran downstairs and into the palatial living room. The furniture had been pushed against the walls, the Oriental rugs had been rolled away to create a dance floor. Helium balloons floated in colorful bunches from every available mooring.

"So, what are your New Year's resolutions, Jess?" Lila asked, tearing open a package of streamers.

Jessica smiled. "Well, it's more of a New Year's prediction," she said. "Michael is going to fall wildly in love with me, for one."

"Yeah, and then after five dates you'll get tired of him and start looking for someone new."

Jessica shrugged and ripped off a piece of tape to attach a streamer to the wall. "Maybe." She jumped off the chair she had been standing on and looked at her friend. "So what's *your* resolution?"

"I don't need to make resolutions," Lila said tossing her long hair behind her shoulders. "I'm already perfect."

Jessica let out a hoot of laughter. "Maybe you should work on being more humble."

Lila paused to consider. "Naah. Humble is for other people. I have a reputation to maintain, you know."

Jessica and Lila burst out laughing. Without a doubt, this was going to be a memorable New Year's Eve.

"Now, hurry up," Lila commanded. "We're not finished yet, and people will be here any minute."

Jessica saluted. "Yes, General Fowler."

Just then, the door bell rang, and Lila let out a shriek. "Party time!" she yelled as she ran for the door.

Jessica finished hanging the streamers. Then she smoothed her dress and followed Lila out into the hall.

Elizabeth checked her watch for the fifteenth time that evening and then glanced at her reflection in the mirror. Todd had come back from Utah just in time for Lila's party, and her heart was beating wildly at the thought of seeing him.

"You look great, Liz," Mrs. Wakefield said, as her daughter walked into the living room. "Todd will fall down in a dead faint when he sees you."

Elizabeth laughed. "He will *not*, Mom. But thanks anyway." She knew she looked great in her short white skirt and blue silk blouse, but it was flattering to hear her mother say so. She paced back and forth a few times and then stopped when she heard a car pull up out front.

"He's here!" she gasped.

Elizabeth flung open the door. Todd was coming up the walkway, and he stopped when he saw her. For a moment, neither moved.

Then Elizabeth flew down the steps and into his arms. Todd spun her around in a tight hug.

"I can't believe you're here!" Elizabeth gazed into his eyes.

He kissed her warmly. "Me, neither. It seems like ages."

"I know," Elizabeth agreed. "So much happened while you were gone."

"How's Enid?" he asked.

They twined their fingers together and walked back to the house. "She's OK," Elizabeth said. "She's been taking it easy at home since the accident, but she promised she'd go to Lila and Jessica's party."

Todd looked deeply into Elizabeth's eyes. "It's so great to see you," he said huskily.

Elizabeth's heart leapt the way it always did when she realized just how much she loved him. It seemed crazy that she had been in such a turmoil over Jeffrey. It had all been a misunderstanding—Elizabeth misunderstanding her own feelings. She knew that she loved Todd completely and that she always would.

"I love you," she said softly.

They kissed again and broke apart only when they heard Mr. Wakefield clearing his throat.

"Hi, Mr. Wakefield," Todd said with a quick smile. "Happy New Year."

"Same to you, Todd," Elizabeth's father said fondly. "Now, you two be careful tonight. There are plenty of crazy people on the roads this time of the year."

Elizabeth ran past her father to get her purse and stopped to give him a quick kiss on the cheek. "You don't need to tell us, Dad. Believe me, we'll be extra careful. I'll be home about one, OK?"

"Fine. Have a good time, sweetie."

When Elizabeth and Todd arrived at Fowler Crest, lights blazed from every window and there were already dozens of cars parked in the driveway.

"Looks like the whole school is here," Elizabeth said.

Todd reached for her hand. "We don't *have* to go in," he said, his eyes sparkling.

"Yes, we do." Elizabeth laughed. She was

happy to think that Todd wanted to be only with her. "Come on. It's New Year's Eve!"

He let out a dramatic sigh. "Yeah, and as soon as we get inside, half of the guys will ask you to dance, and I won't get to see you all night."

"That's not true and you know it." Elizabeth leaned over to kiss him and then whispered in his ear, "I won't dance with anyone but you tonight, deal?"

"Deal."

Elizabeth felt wonderful. Hand in hand, she and Todd walked up the broad steps and let themselves inside. Jessica was dancing with Michael in the huge foyer. She broke away from him when she spotted Elizabeth and Todd.

"You're here!" she sang out. "Happy New Year! You have to wear a funny hat, you know. They're in the living room."

Before they could answer, Jessica ran back to Michael.

"I see that nothing's changed since I've been away," Todd said, grinning.

"Some things have," Elizabeth answered, thinking of what had happened between her and Jeffrey. "But most things are just the same." She looked into Todd's eyes, knowing that he understood her perfectly.

                    *   *   *

Jeffrey parked his car and walked up to Lila's house. He had asked Enid to come with him, but she said that she preferred to come separately. Jeffrey knew that she wasn't really turning him down. He knew that she was waiting for him to say something, something more than just "Let's go together to Lila's party."

But with what he had just gone through with Elizabeth, and with what Enid had gone through with her family, Jeffrey knew that neither of them was really ready for a new relationship. Still, Jeffrey cared very much about Enid. He wanted to tell her what he thought when he saw Mr. Rollins dragging her from the wrecked car. At that moment, Jeffrey realized just what a very special person Enid was and how much he valued her. He would hate to risk their friendship by rushing a romance that wasn't ready to begin.

As soon as Jeffrey walked in the door, several of his friends greeted him and called him over to join them. He smiled and waved, but instead of joining them he looked around for Enid. He made his way through the crowd, his eyes searching hopefully.

When Jeffrey reached the living room, he spotted Elizabeth and Todd. They were dancing close, gazing into each other's eyes.

A pang of bittersweet nostalgia shot through Jeffrey as he saw them together. Once, Elizabeth had looked up at him that way.

He's lucky, Jeffrey thought, looking at Todd without jealousy and at Elizabeth without regret.

He smiled and glanced toward the foyer. There was still no sign of Enid. Jeffrey curbed his impatience.

"Hey, Jeffrey," Lila said, waltzing up to him, a party hat in her hand. She placed it on his head and gave him a coquettish smile. "Do you want to dance?"

"Hi, Lila," Jeffrey replied, settling the pointy hat on his head. "Sorry, but I was looking for, uh, someone," he said shyly.

"Typical," Lila said, smiling to take the edge off her tone. "See you later. Hope you find her."

Jeffrey grinned and headed back to the front hall. He was going to be there, waiting, when Enid walked in.

Enid walked slowly down the hall and looked into the living room. "I'm leaving, Mom."

207

Mrs. Rollins looked up from her book. "Oh, Enid. You look so nice!"

"I do?" Enid asked, twirling around happily. "Thanks. And look what I'm wearing," she added, holding up her heart pendant.

"The bracelet your father gave you looks perfect with it."

Enid fingered the delicate gold chain around her wrist. Thinking of her father brought a smile to her face.

"And, Mom, I want you to know that you don't have to worry about me tonight," she added. "I can celebrate New Year's Eve without doing anything dumb. I feel a lot better about you and Dad—and about myself."

Mrs. Rollins stood up and walked over to her daughter. "I know I can trust you, sweetheart. Just be careful on the road."

"I will." Enid kissed her mother's cheek and then grabbed her purse and the keys to the car. Tonight she would see her friends for the first time since that sunny Christmas morning. People had called—particularly Elizabeth and Jeffrey —but she had used her physical recuperation as an excuse to be alone for a while. She hadn't wanted to talk to anyone until she had some things straightened out in her mind.

Enid had spent a great deal of time thinking.

She realized that in the days right before Christmas she had allowed feelings of loneliness and self-pity to overwhelm her. Instead of being honest with her parents, Elizabeth, and Jeffrey, she had hidden her anger, and it had turned against her. In the past week, she had come to terms with her parents. Now it was time to come to terms with her friends—and with Brian.

Brian had called during the week from the burn unit. When Enid heard his voice on the phone, she had been tempted to hang up. But the tone of Brian's voice was tentative, even hopeful, and she had stayed on the line. Brian told her that he had spoken with her father and had thanked him for saving his life. He had been doing a lot of thinking and realized how vulnerable he still was to pressure from his friends. He was sorry for having forced Enid to party with him on Christmas Eve, and he was even more sorry that he had put her life in danger. He knew he had hurt her and he didn't expect to be forgiven. Mr. Rollins and the doctor had talked to him about getting some help from a counselor or a rehabilitation center after he was released from the hospital, and Brian's parents were already checking out some places.

As Enid listened to Brian, she couldn't help but feel sorry for him. She knew he wasn't really a bad person. She hoped he would find the courage to feel good about himself without having to drink or take drugs. Brian told her that he would be in the hospital for quite a while, and Enid was planning to visit him sometime in the next week. Brian probably needed some friends right now, and Enid knew how valuable friends were in times of trouble.

Now, as she got ready to leave the house, Enid thought of her friend Jeffrey. When Jeffrey had asked her to go with him to Lila and Jessica's party, Enid had wanted to say yes. But she also needed to know just how he really felt about her. She realized that she was no longer completely sure of her own feelings for Jeffrey. But they would talk, and they would find out together.

Her heartbeat quickened as she drove up the hill to Fowler Crest. New Year's Eve was a good night for rejoining her friends. It was a night of new beginnings, new resolutions. And with a surge of excitement, she realized that she really did have a lot to look forward to.

Enid paused on the doorstep, listening to the music and the laughter. How would her friends react when she walked through that door? Would they be thinking of how drunk she had been, what a fool she had made of herself? Would they whisper and turn away from her?

Some of them might, she decided. *But Elizabeth won't. Jeffrey won't.* She was even pretty confident that Jessica and Lila wouldn't, either.

Enid knew now that she could handle whatever happened with her own strength, and with the support of her friends and her family. Never again would she have to hide her fears or her pain in drugs or alcohol.

After taking a deep breath, Enid rang the bell. To her surprise Jeffrey opened it, and his face lit up when he saw her.

"You made it!" he exclaimed as she entered the foyer.

Enid knew that she wasn't imagining his happiness at seeing her.

"Hi," she whispered.

"How do you feel?" Jeffrey's green eyes were warm and admiring. "You look great."

"So do you," she admitted, gazing up at him.

"Come on. Let's dance. I've been sitting here waiting for you for ages!"

Enid followed Jeffrey into the living room, where she was greeted by a chorus of hellos and with warm, welcoming smiles. Not one person looked at her accusingly.

"Enid!" Elizabeth shouted over the music and laughter.

"Hi, Enid. How are you?" Todd asked as he and Elizabeth joined them.

"I'm great, Todd. How was your trip?" Enid asked.

"Fantastic!"

Elizabeth looked from Enid to Jeffrey and back again with a smile that betrayed not a trace of jealousy or anxiety.

"Do you want to dance?" Jeffrey asked, taking her elbow.

"See you later," Enid said to Todd and Elizabeth. From that moment on, Jeffrey never left her side. They danced and talked and walked outside under the stars. Jeffrey was warm and funny and complimentary, and Enid felt better than she had in ages. They were standing on the terrace when they heard the music stop and a muffled chanting take its place.

Enid gasped. "Is it midnight already?"

Jeffrey held his arm up to peer at his watch in the darkness. "Almost."

"Should we go in?" Enid asked, taking a step.

"Why don't we stay out here," Jeffrey suggested, reaching for her hand. His voice was hoarse with emotion when he continued. "Enid —I think—"

"Wait," Enid interrupted, her heart pounded. She wanted them to take things slowly. "Let's take it one day at a time," she whispered.

He laughed softly. "Are you sure?"

"Positive." Enid smiled at him and took a step closer. "But you could give me a New Year's Eve kiss, you know."

"I'll do my best." Jeffrey bent his head to kiss her.

"Happy New Year," Enid murmured. The future was as bright as the full moon shining down on them.

COULD *YOU* BE THE NEXT SWEET VALLEY READER OF THE MONTH?

ENTER BANTAM BOOKS' SWEET VALLEY CONTEST & SWEEPSTAKES IN ONE!

Calling all Sweet Valley Fans! Here's a chance to appear in a Sweet Valley book!

We know how important Sweet Valley is to you. That's why we've come up with a Sweet Valley celebration offering exciting opportunities to have YOUR thoughts printed in a Sweet Valley book!

"How do I become a Sweet Valley Reader of the Month?"

It's easy. Just write a one-page essay (no more than 150 words, please) telling us a little about yourself, and why you like to read Sweet Valley books. We will pick the best essays and print them along with the winner's photo in the back of upcoming Sweet Valley books. Every month there will be a new Sweet Valley High Reader of the Month!

And, there's more!

Just sending in your essay makes you eligible for the Grand Prize drawing for a trip to Los Angeles, California! This once-in-a-life-time trip includes round-trip airfare, accommodations for 5 nights (economy double occupancy), a rental car, and meal allowances. (Approximate retail value: $4,500.)

Don't wait! Write your essay today.
No purchase necessary. See the next page for Official rules.

ENTER BANTAM BOOKS' SWEET-VALLEY READER OF THE MONTH SWEEPSTAKES

OFFICIAL RULES:

READER OF THE MONTH ESSAY CONTEST

1. No Purchase Is Necessary. Enter by hand printing your name, address, date of birth and telephone number on a plain 3" x 5" card, and sending this card along with your essay telling us about yourself and why you like to read Sweet Valley books to:

READER OF THE MONTH
SWEET VALLEY HIGH
BANTAM BOOKS
YR MARKETING
666 FIFTH AVENUE
NEW YORK, NEW YORK 10103

2. Reader of the Month Contest Winner. For each month from June 1, 1990 through December 31, 1990, a Sweet Valley High Reader of the Month will be chosen from the entries received during that month. The winners will have their essay and photo published in the back of an upcoming Sweet Valley High title.

3. Enter as often as you wish, but each essay must be original and each entry must be mailed in a separate envelope bearing sufficient postage. All completed entries must be postmarked and received by Bantam no later than December 31, 1990, in order to be eligible for the Essay Contest and Sweepstakes. Entrants must be between the ages of 6 and 16 years old. Each essay must be no more than 150 words and must be typed double-spaced or neatly printed on one side of an 8 1/2" x 11" page which has the entrant's name, address, date of birth and telephone number at the top. The essays submitted will be judged each month by Bantam's Marketing Department on the basis of originality, creativity, thoughtfulness, and writing ability, and all of Bantam's decisions are final and binding. Essays become the property of Bantam Books and none will be returned. Bantam reserves the right to edit the winning essays for length and readability. Essay Contest winners will be notified by mail within 30 days of being chosen. In the event there are an insufficient number of essays received in any month which meet the minimum standards established by the judges, Bantam reserves the right not to choose a Reader of the Month. Winners have 30 days from the date of Bantam's notice in which to respond, or an alternate Reader of the Month winner will be chosen. Bantam is not responsible for incomplete or lost or misdirected entries.

4. Winners of the Essay Contest and their parents or legal guardians may be required to execute an Affidavit of Eligibility and Promotional Release supplied by Bantam. Entering the Reader of the Month Contest constitutes permission for use of the winner's name, address, likeness and contest submission for publicity and promotional purposes, with no additional compensation.

5. Employees of Bantam Books, Bantam Doubleday Dell Publishing Group, Inc., and

their subsidiaries and affiliates, and their immediate family members are not eligible to enter the Essay Contest. The Essay Contest is open to residents of the U.S. and Canada (excluding the province of Quebec), and is void wherever prohibited or restricted by law. All applicable federal, state, and local regulations apply.

READER OF THE MONTH SWEEPSTAKES

6. Sweepstakes Entry. No purchase is necessary. Every entrant in the Sweet Valley High, Sweet Valley Twins and Sweet Valley Kids Essay Contest whose completed entry is received by December 31, 1990 will be entered in the Reader of the Month Sweepstakes. The Grand Prize winner will be selected in a random drawing from all completed entries received on or about February 1, 1991 and will be notified by mail. Bantam's decision is final and binding. Odds of winning are dependent on the number of entries received. The prize is non-transferable and no substitution is allowed. The Grand Prize winner must be accompanied on the trip by a parent or legal guardian. Taxes are the sole responsibility of the prize winner. Trip must be taken within one year of notification and is subject to availability. Travel arrangements will be made for the winner and, once made, no changes will be allowed.

7. 1 Grand Prize. A six day, five night trip for two to Los Angeles, California. Includes round-trip coach airfare, accommodations for 5 nights (economy double occupancy), a rental car – economy model, and spending allowance for meals. (Approximate retail value: $4,500.)

8. The Grand Prize winner and their parent or legal guardian may be required to execute an Affidavit of Eligibility and Promotional Release supplied by Bantam. Entering the Reader of the Month Sweepstakes constitutes permission for use of the winner's name, address, and the likeness for publicity and promotional purposes, with no additional compensation.

9. Employees of Bantam Books, Bantam Doubleday Dell Publishing Group, Inc., and their subsidiaries and affiliates, and their immediate family members are not eligible to enter this Sweepstakes. The Sweepstakes is open to residents of the U.S. and Canada (excluding the province of Quebec), and is void wherever prohibited or restricted by law. If a Canadian resident, the Grand Prize winner will be required to correctly answer an arithmetical skill-testing question in order to receive the prize. All applicable federal, state, and local regulations apply. The Grand Prize will be awarded in the name of the minor's parent or guardian. Taxes, if any, are the winner's sole responsibility.

10. For the name of the Grand Prize winner and the names of the winners of the Sweet Valley High, Sweet Valley Twins and Sweet Valley Kids Essay Contests, send a stamped, self-addressed envelope entirely separate from your entry to: Bantam Books, Sweet Valley Reader of the Month Winners, Young Readers Marketing, 666 Fifth Avenue, New York, New York 10103. The winners list will be available after April 15, 1991.

MURDER AND MYSTERY STRIKES

America's favorite teen series has a hot new line of
Super Thrillers!

It's super excitement, super suspense, and super thrills as Jessica and Elizabeth Wakefield put on their detective caps in the new SWEET VALLEY HIGH SUPER THRILLERS! Follow these two sleuths as they witness a murder...find themselves running from the mob...and uncover the dark secrets of a mysterious woman. SWEET VALLEY HIGH SUPER THRILLERS are guaranteed to keep you on the edge of your seat!

YOU'LL WANT TO READ THEM ALL!

- ❏ #1: DOUBLE JEOPARDY   26905-4/$2.95
- ❏ #2: ON THE RUN   27230-6/$2.95
- ❏ #3: NO PLACE TO HIDE   27554-2/$2.95
- ❏ #4: DEADLY SUMMER   28010-4/$2.95

HAVE YOU READ THE LATEST!
SWEET VALLEY STARS

- ❏ #1: LILA'S STORY   28296-4/$2.95
- ❏ #2: BRUCE'S STORY   28464-9/$2.95
- ❏ #3: ENID'S STORY   28576-9/$2.95

Bantam Books, Dept. SVH5, 414 East Golf Road, Des Plaines, IL 60016

Please send me the items I have checked above. I am enclosing $_____ (please add $2.00 to cover postage and handling). Send check or money order, no cash or C.O.D.s please.

Mr/Ms _____

Address _____

City/State _____ Zip_____

SVH5-12/90

Please allow four to six weeks for delivery.
Prices and availability subject to change without notice.

Celebrate the Seasons
with SWEET VALLEY HIGH
Super Editions

You've been a SWEET VALLEY HIGH fan all along—
hanging out with Jessica and Elizabeth and their friends
at Sweet Valley High. And now the SWEET VALLEY
HIGH *Super Editions* give you more of what you like
best—more romance—more excitement—more real-life
adventure! Whether you're bicycling up the California
Coast in PERFECT SUMMER, dancing at the Sweet
Valley Christmas Ball in SPECIAL CHRISTMAS, touring
the South of France in SPRING BREAK, catching the
rays in a MALIBU SUMMER, or skiing the snowy slopes
in WINTER CARNIVAL—you know you're exactly
where you want to be—with the gang from SWEET
VALLEY HIGH.

SWEET VALLEY HIGH SUPER EDITIONS

☐ **PERFECT SUMMER**
25072/$2.95

☐ **MALIBU SUMMER**
26050/$2.95

☐ **SPRING BREAK**
25537/$2.95

☐ **WINTER CARNIVAL**
26159/$2.95

☐ **SPECIAL CHRISTMAS**
25377/$2.95

☐ **SPRING FEVER**
26420/$2.95